Delhi
via
Lucknow

**Once love travelled
this route...**

ASHWINI RUDRA

Leadstart
INKSTATE

ISBN: 978-93-5610-607-9

First published in India 2022 by Leadstart Inkstate
A brand of One Point Six Technologies Pvt. Ltd.

123, Building J2, Shram Seva Premises,
Wadala Truck Terminal,
Mumbai 400022, Maharashtra, INDIA
Phone: +91 96999 33000
Email: info@leadstartcorp.com
www.leadstartcorp.com

Disclaimer: This is a work of fiction. All the names, characters, businesses, places, events and incidents in this book are either the product of the author's imagination or used in a fictitious manner. Any resemblance to actual persons, living or dead, or actual events is purely coincidental.

Editor: Shayoni Mitra
Cover: Komal Kohok
Layouts: Kevis Tech

I dedicate it to all,
I dedicate it to none,
I dedicate it to you,
and to the person who is the only ONE.

I thank everyone,
I thank you all,
special thanks to the people,
who all laughed when Humpty had a great fall.

There was a time I wanted to write a novel. Later, I wrote one, but by that time, my life itself had become a novel. Before you begin to read, I want to share a bit of funny advice. Trust me, Bollywoodish romance is injurious to your well-being. Never try to mimic it. Don't try to bend your knees and tilt your body a little like the 'king of romance' of Bollywood, SRK. You will fail. You will *fall*.

Falling is good... you learn how to stand, and then, you allow others to smile. Here I'm presenting a story – a *desi* young adult novel. I hope, after reading this you are going to smile, because, I always fall. I fall in love with readers like you...

Life is short. Smiling is one of the most precious emotions we render in this short life. So, smile at me and at every character of this novel. In life, eventually, all emotions merge into one, and stories run through it.
Happy reading.

"Air India Flight AI411 from Lucknow to Delhi is delayed by three hours."

Mir Taqi Mir would not have been able to write a single line at modern airports if he had been subjected to the raucous 'noise' made by the female announcer. Or wait, a great poet of the stature of Mir would be able to write couplets anywhere and in any situation. Himanshu should not judge his capabilities.

Himanshu took a long stride to reach the Indian Airlines gate at Chaudhary Charan Singh International Airport. He had bought a sandwich from a multinational burger joint. The aroma of Aloo Tikki burger, cheese and mayonnaise filled his nose.

He noticed the song playing on a TV. An Indian hip-hop star was singing about running a party till four in the morning. The singer was afraid that an aunty could call the police. Oh, dear Mir! You would not have been able to endure these lyrics or poetry. It was good that Mir had met his demise a couple of hundred years ago.

Himanshu looked at his watch, a gift from his wife on their fifth wedding anniversary. It was 10 am. He crossed his leg anxiously on an uncomfortable iron chair. Seeing a celebrity gossip magazine on the stall, he picked it up and, flipping through, noticed an article about Ajay Devgan. It brought a smile, but this vanished soon due to the numbness in his leg.

He looked at his dark blue suit pants. They were a little dusty. Growing annoyed, he cursed the chair. He bent and leaned forward but then sat back again; cleaning and dusting his bottom in public was not a clever idea.

He played with his mobile and looked at text alerts. He read the text message. It was from Sanaya. '*Miss you a lot! I have checked the flight status. It's late.*'

He typed back, '*It has been ten years, but it seems like day one of our marriage. I will not miss your birthday. See you soon.*'

He scrolled through his WhatsApp messages and saw a profile he had saved as "Bechu Mishra." There was a grim-looking face of Bechu in his profile, which Himanshu had clicked forcefully. Himanshu dialled the number.

The phone rang thrice, and Bechu picked up the phone. "Hello, Guddu. *Kaisey yaad kiya?*"

"*Mishra Ji,* Happy birthday," Himanshu said.

"I know, it's easy for you. Sanaya and I share the same birthday."

"Yes, and this evening I'm throwing a small party at Tito's. You have to join."

"Sure, but I can sniff that you are smiling. What's cooking?"

"Nothing, just a picture of Ajay Devgan in a magazine," Himanshu said, unable to control his laughter.

"Bugger. You have not forgotten anything."

"How could I forget, man? It's about our first love. We fancied the same girl."

"Yes, I know, but you are married now. Control your urges."

"Mr Charted Accountant, reminiscing about your first love is not cheating," Himanshu grinned. "I married and moved on, but you are still stuck. Sulking. You are thirty-eight. Find a suitable girl and get married."

"Yep, then find a suitable girl for me. I could not marry my first love because of you… and now I'm unlucky and cannot find any! No one is like Rimjhim." Bechu had hesitated before saying the name and faking a laugh. Within a second, his heart filled with memories, like all good old times, reverie comes with a pang of pain. It pierces your heart like a poisoned needle.

"Shut up. Why don't you join Sanskrit classes again? Probably you will find your dream girl there," Himanshu smirked.

"Can you stop teasing me? I have a meeting with a client. See you at Tito's," Bechu said in a hurry.

Before he could hang up, Himanshu said, "As I promised, I will find a girl for you," then he heard a click sound. Bechu had cut the phone without listening to his last words.

Himanshu sighed. The announcer's voice echoed. He started thinking about Mir again. There had been a time he used to read and recite Mir. But then he fell in love. To impress a girl in the nineties, English was one of the necessities. It still was. He had started listening to bands like Backstreet Boys and Boyzone. His friends used to worship Altaf Raja. Mir hid in the corner of his heart. Now he was ashamed of this idiotic comparison. The stories of our adolescence are always funny.

✳

When there is a delay, there is hunger. Himanshu bought a veg patty from a pastry store and came back to the same iron chair. He checked his expensive watch; he still had one and half hours to pass. He looked for a bar. In India, they don't serve alcohol in the airspace. Probably, airlines in India stopped this practice because of a large number of misbehaving incidents with air-hostesses. We Indians have a low tolerance for alcohol but a high tolerance for boorish behaviour. Guddu knew that in the airport there was a bar. The Lounge.

At Lounge, there were few options available. There was a young girl attendant at the bar. She gave a curt smile to Himanshu just to show a fake inclination towards the motto 'atithi devo bhava'. Clearly, she didn't care much about her job.

"A glass of pinot noir," Guddu said, but then thought again. "In fact, do you have Kingfisher? I don't feel like drinking wine today."

"Yes, sir!" The girl was confused for a moment, and then she turned to get Himanshu's drink.

"Get two cans please," said Himanshu. He had to fly and it was better to get tipsy and get some sleep. He had some tiring financial meetings this week.

The girl came back with a beer tankard with foam floating on the top. The sweet molasses smell brought enough memories to reverberate. Himanshu gulped it.

The waitress put the second can down beside the tankard, which Himanshu slipped into his pocket. He glazed down the beer mug, paid the bill and then strode back to his assigned gate.

A sleek, slender girl approached gracefully and placed her stroller bag on the seat across from his. Himanshu could not see her face, but he could smell the peculiar scent. He could feel her.

He started murmuring to himself, "Don't turn. Hell, it cannot be you! It cannot be you!"

His heart was thumping. With a trembling hand, he withdrew a handkerchief and wiped the stream of sweat from his forehead. Every heartbeat was echoing the woman's name. She was in a turquoise *saree*, standing in front of him.

The woman turned and took her seat. Himanshu's world slowed down as if he had smoked a whole joint of weed. His ears became red. This woman was Rimjhim. The same Rimjhim because of whom he had moved from Lucknow to Kanpur. The Rimjhim because of whom Himanshu had flunked his MBA entrance exams for three consecutive years. Rimjhim, the reason he had quit his political life.

Himanshu began looking at the gate. He was nervous and unsure of what he should do. He stood and picked up his bag. He decided to walk away, unnoticed. Then he realized he had never been a coward in his life. He had always faced every situation like a lion, with confidence. He had lived his life like the Guddu *Bhaiya*. Yes, that was what he was. By profession, he was Himanshu Shukla, an executive officer of a multinational company. But in his heart, he was still Guddu. His past was sitting in front of him, and he had to face it like Guddu Shukla. That was his name.

Guddu, aka Himanshu, took a deep breath and threw his brown sling leather bag on the iron chair.

A crackling metal sound disturbed Rimjhim's concentration. She closed the novel she was reading and looked up. She gasped. She could not believe it. Her old stalker was standing in front of her.

"Don't worry, it has been seventeen years, and I'm not stalking you! Now don't say you don't recognize me," Guddu said.

He wanted to say, "Seventeen years, five months, and some sixteen days," like a line of cheesy dialogue in an SRK movie. But he chose not to do so, as he was in fact unaware of the exact number of months and days it had been.

"No, I don't recognize you," Rimjhim said.

"Oh!" Guddu thought for a moment, and then he tilted his neck to the right, like Ajay Devgan. He had just had cheese with the burger, so it would be best to flush it out of his body while mimicking the cheesy style of the actor.

"Oh. Stop it, Guddu. It was because of the outfit that I didn't recognize you. I know you were an Ajay Devgan fan." She laughed. Her fear had evaporated in a second. "For years and years, I have envisioned the stalker Guddu in a *mawaali* look: black pants, check shirt with a top button open. You used to chew gutkha all the time. How could I recognize you in this banker look!"

"An investment banker, I'll have you know, and I think my salt and pepper look resembles George Clooney." Guddu sat down next to her. He tried to be funny. Girls like funny people. Whether they love them or not, however, was a different topic.

Rimjhim felt uncomfortable. She moved a bit, adjusted herself. Her lips quivered. She squeezed the novel tightly, folding it in half, and frowned. She looked toward the gate and duty-free shops, unaware of how to proceed with the conversation. There was an awkward silence for a few seconds, then she said, "For a minute, I was scared."

"I know, but don't worry. I'm a happily married man," Guddu said, showing his ring finger.

"What's her name?"

"Sanaya."

"And kids?"

"In the process," Guddu smiled.

"Congratulations!"

"No, she is not pregnant. I meant we are trying." Guddu blushed. Here he was, discussing his sex life with his crush. Not crush, he should say 'love'. Some may have said 'infatuation'.

Guddu noticed airline staff, stewards, and stewardesses. They had assembled at the gate and were waiting for the pilot. Guddu checked the time. There was still an hour and a half till boarding.

Guddu looked at Rimjhim. She was still as beautiful as she had been seventeen years ago. It was as if she had not aged by even a day... no wrinkles, and her face was still glowing. Tiny studs in her ears and the nose-ring glittered and these flashes were ready to skip his heartbeat.

Ignoring Guddu, Rimjhim returned to reading her novel. For the first time in Guddu's life, he saw her at ease.

"I owe this banker look to you," Guddu tried to initiate conversation again.

"How so?" Rimjhim looked up at him, interested.

"Well, to impress you, I wanted to do an MBA to become a banker."

"What! Then why the hell did you chew tobacco and fight like a goon? You also used to carry that locally made pistol," Rimjhim said. "Was that also to impress me?"

"I was in my early twenties," Guddu replied sheepishly. "And aren't you girls impressed by bad guys?"

"Hell no!"

"Don't lie. You all want a bad boy. A man who can protect you."

"You guys don't know what we want; we want a gentleman who can protect us, not a *mawaa*..." Rimjhim paused. It was the second time she was referring to Guddu as a '*mawaali*'.

She looked at Guddu, who was now a gentleman. She smiled and concluded her sentence, "*Mawaali, gunda.*"

"A gentleman who can protect his woman? That's a euphemism for a *mawaali!*" Guddu laughed.

"Euphemism! What?"

"Nothing, you won't get it. My jokes are becoming stupid with my age." Himanshu tousled his hair and looked at the glass across the front of the duty-free shop. He was forty, and he was getting old.

Himanshu heard the voice of the female announcer again – time had flown like a rocket.

"Where are you going?" he asked.

"Delhi. We are on the same flight; that is why we are at the same gate."

Himanshu felt stupid. Girls are good at connecting dots and comprehending situations.

"It's time to board. I'm flying business class, so I'll be boarding first. Can we meet at Delhi Airport? For a cup of coffee? That is if your husband won't mind."

"Sure, see you in Delhi. But why do you assume that I can't travel business class? Do I look like an economy class girl to you now?"

"No. Your killer look still kills thousands of boys of Kanpur."

"Stop flirting!" Rimjhim blushed.

"What's your seat number?" Himanshu asked.

"11 A."

"Nice, window seat. Anyways, see you later."

Guddu adjusted his bag on his right shoulder and walked towards the gate to board. For a moment, he considered asking the stewardess to give him 11B. Any middle seat guy would have been ready to exchange a business class window seat. But then Guddu looked at his mobile screensaver of Sanaya and dumped this idea.

＊

The captain's husky voice came over the intercom, informing the passengers of the weather in Delhi. Guddu gave his coat to the stewardess and adjusted his seat. He looked towards the stewards, who were getting ready for an in-flight safety demonstration. Why do all pilots in the world have that baritone voice? Maybe they get training for this to attract more people to this profession. This kind of voice always reminded him of Sunil Chauhan, the tall guy from Meerut. He knew how to play the love game.

The flight took off, and Guddu pressed a button. An air-hostess arrived wearing a fake smile.

"A glass of water," Guddu said.

Guddu looked back to seat 11A. He could see Rimjhim. He waited for a few seconds hoping that Rimjhim would look at him, but life is not a '*palat*' sequence of *DDLJ*. The air-hostess arrived in a minute with a glass of water. Guddu picked the hidden Kingfisher can and gulped it down. He squinted out of the window. The swirling clouds wove his past story. It was the story of Guddu's arch-rival, Bechu, and their mutual love interest, Rimjhim.

It was the time when the nineties had made the transition to the millennium, but the essence of nineties pop-culture was present. It was the time when the Jennifer Lopez song 'Waiting for tonight' was considered a little bold. It was so racy that small-town parents had concerns that MTV was impacting *Bharatiya Sanskriti* at that time... A time when carrying a big bulky mobile phone was a fashion symbol; the bigger the mobile phone, the higher one's status in society. It was also the time when studying commerce was a sign of a weak student. Then, he was twenty-three years old.

Guddu had embarked on an M.Sc. in Chemistry to disguise his weakness. He had a gap of a couple of years in his education. His student life was filled with ebbs and flows. With flashes, his memory travelled the lane of Ganga Ghats at Bithoor, DAV College at Civil Lines, Barra, Lal-Imli Churaha, and Kanpur Sangrahalaya. He remembered streets full of messy electrical wires. It was still fresh in his mind how he had helped, showing his '*kattiyabazi*' skill to a *theka* owner at Kanpur-Jhansi Highway near Barra. He was regular at this local bar.

Kanpur, March 2003

The bar owner was playing the song of the century: '*Jeeta tha jiske liye, jiske liye marta tha*'. Guddu heard the song. He began to pound on the battered table.

"Who is playing this song?" Guddu screamed. He picked up an empty Kingfisher bottle and scratched his shoulder.

A tremor rippled through the bar. The customers, primarily daily wages workers, looked at Guddu. They were terrified. The bar owner trembled.

"I have stopped it, *Guddu Bhaiya*," the owner said apologetically as he removed a cassette from the player, placing it in the Dilwale cassette cover. Ajay Devgan looked grim on the cover, and Raveena Tandon, the actress, tried to look as bubbly as possible.

"*Guddu Bhaiya*, this is Kanpur, not Lucknow," Uma murmured.

"I know, I know. I was testing whether you are drunk or not. But it looks like you all are drunk. Why else would you be playing this song, which romanticizes the past? I'm still in love. It's not *jeeta tha jiske liye*; I'm still living for her," Guddu said as he thumped the table.

Scanning the bar and ogling at some posters of B-grade Hindi movies stars, Guddu took his wallet from his pocket and handed five thousand rupees to the owner.

"Improve the standard of this bar; remove these posters. It does not look good."

"Sure, *Guddu Bhaiya*. I will play ghazals next time," the bar owner stammered. Then he counted the fresh notes and grinned, showing the red tint of his teeth from years of chewing *paan*.

"No, play Venga Boys. I'm preparing for my MBA. I am trying to improve my English."

Uma and Sunil, Guddu's two henchmen, were impressed. *Guddu Bhaiya* had a knack for English, and he could crack the CAT this year for sure.

Guddu picked up the keys to his Jeep and moved forward. He reached the wooden gate and turned to glance at Uma.

Uma picked 500 bucks back from the bundle of notes from the bar owner's hand.

"Buy some Back Street Boys too. *Bhaiya* has memorized 'Quit Playing Games with My Heart'," Uma advised the owner.

Sunil picked up a half-finished bottle and gulped it in a hurry.

The daily wages workers gasped.

"He must be a spoilt brat," a worker muttered, rubbing *khaini*, tobacco, in his palm.

"Shhh! *Tumhari maiyya-bappa ek kar dega.* He is *the Guddu Bhaiya*," the owner shushed the worker. He took a pinch of tobacco from the worker's hand and placed it beneath his lip.

✳

An open Jeep was slithering through an empty road in Kanpur late at night.

Uma combed his curly hair and looked at Guddu, but hesitated. He then pulled at his blue jeans, trying to stretch the crotch, and then he adjusted his seat.

"Why the hell do you wear these shitty jeans? Wear tailored pants. It's more comfortable. It goes well with *Kolhapuri chappals*," Guddu glared at Uma. He noticed that Uma's eyes were glittering with some wicked ideas. "You want to tell me something?" Guddu asked.

"*Bhaiya*, as Sunil is new, he should know," said Uma while sniffing the midnight air.

"Know what?"

"He needs orientation. Which girls he can pursue, and which he cannot."

Guddu took a sharp turn, and his tyres screeched as a motorbike rushed from the opposite direction. He berated the biker. *Madhar...*

The smell of burning rubber filled Sunil's nostrils. He got out to check the Jeep's tyres, but could not see any problems.

"Don't talk like that. I will cut the guy into pieces if he stalks Rimjhim!" Guddu yelled.

Pale-faced Sunil swallowed his spit. He looked to Uma for help. Umanath gestured to Sunil that things were under control.

"*Bhaiya*, easy. I meant anyone could do it by mistake. After all, both sisters are so beautiful. It's my duty to protect *Bhabhi Ji*."

"*Chutiye*, she does not need your protection. She is a *Kshatriya*, a warrior."

Guddu drew a wallet from his pocket and tossed it at Sunil who had gotten back into the rear seat. "Look at this pic Sunil. Her name is Rimjhim. You are new to the university, so you should know that you are supposed to bow with respect. She is your *Bhabhi*."

Sunil fumbled but managed to open the wallet. He saw a coloured photo of a girl who was probably in her early twenties. She was slender and had black straight hair. In the photo, she looked a little scared. Sunil nodded his head. His tipsiness was gone, and he was back to his senses. Fear can make the effects of drinks or drugs evaporate in an instance. And if a drunk *purabiya* guy is talking, with a pistol tucked in his trousers, one ought to be scared. Sunil returned the wallet to Guddu with a trembling hand.

"Do you know why this wannabe IITian, the district topper of 1999, Uma Nath Pandey, is worried? He likes Rimjhim's younger sister, Rakshita," Guddu said.

He looked at Sunil Chauhan again and reached to place his hands on his shoulders. Sunil ducked, assuming that a slap was coming in his way.

"Her name is Rakshita Singh," Guddu continued. "This guy wants to get a glimpse of her. After all, he is a Romeo." Guddu cast a disgusted glance at Uma's way, then revved the Jeep on the Kanpur-Jhansi Highway.

After midnight, Guddu stopped his Jeep in front of a pitch dark, deserted alley.

Rubbing his eyes, Sunil read a few signs. It was Pant Nagar. He looked at Uma, who snored in the front seat. Two stray dogs came out from the alley, growled at Sunil, and disappeared into the darkness.

"Even dogs of the alley are warriors. That is the kind of vibe Rimjhim has," Guddu said and turned towards Uma. He patted his back.

"Get up, champion. We are at our in-laws' place." Guddu pointed at a stray dog. It was barking at the nook of Pant Nagar's alley.

"*Bhaiya Ji*, I like your sense of humour," Sunil muttered to Guddu, smiling.

Uma jumped out of the Jeep. He grabbed a mineral water bottle, poured some water on his hollowed palm, and splashed it on his eyes.

"Guddu *bhaiya*, I will be back. Do you want to join?" Uma asked.

"I'm not a *champak aashiq* like you," Guddu glared.

Uma walked towards the alley. He passed three houses, and stray dogs started following him. They were growling at every step Uma took. But under the influence of alcohol, Uma did not realize their unfriendliness.

"Guddu *Bhaiya*, even the dogs are welcoming us to our in-laws' neighbourhood," Uma screamed.

He strolled ahead and came to a stop in front of a house. He read the house board: Shatrughan Singh – Contractor. Uma turned towards Guddu and squinted. He could see the Jeep in the blurry light of street lamps. Uma waved and gave a victorious smile.

Guddu gestured for Sunil to get into the front seat.

"You were amazed by my sense of humour, now enjoy the act of a drunk guy." Guddu laughed and lit a cigarette. He turned on the Jeep radio and searched through the channels. "*De de pyaar de*," a song from the movie *Sharabi*, swelled in the background. Guddu noticed that some lights came on in a few houses, and residents opened their windows to look outside.

On the other side, ignorant and tipsy Uma, hearing the song, got courage. He spread his hands like Bollywood actor Shahrukh Khan and screamed in Amitabh's voice, "*Rakshita meri jaan*, where are you? Here comes your beloved! Come out."

A few more lights came on in the houses. Many people started peeping out of their windows to see who was screaming. Uma was still amazed by his bravery and standing like a "man." Then he heard the ear-splitting sound of two girls. They screamed. It must be Rimjhim and Rakshita. Uma listened to a manly voice. It rumbled, *madharchod*. Uma was in trouble.

"Get the hell out of here. Contractor Saheb is mad," Guddu screamed from the other end.

Shatrughan Singh, a tall and stout man, rushed out from his big iron gate with a double-barrelled rifle. The contracting business had taught him how to deal with these nuisances. Huffing and puffing, he growled, "Who the hell dares to come to my front door and call my daughter!"

The so-called friendly dogs also became rogue. They chased Uma. Uma sprinted faster than Usain Bolt. "Guddu *Bhaiya*, start the Jeep."

"If you are a son of a real man, if you have real courage, then come back, and I will bury you beneath the streets of Kanpur. I will slap you so hard that you *chutiyas* will bounce like a basketball," Shatrughan Singh shouted.

He took his rifle and aimed into the darkness. He shot, and a spark hit the electricity pole with a boom. A few neighbours came out from their houses and stared at Shatrughan. They were not happy.

Guddu started his Jeep. Uma ran and jumped in. He panted, and his heart raced. Guddu gunned the engine and drove away.

Shatrughan Singh frowned at the Jeep till the red backlight disappeared in the darkness.

✳

The Jeep entered DAV boys' hostel, a rickety red building. There were no signs of any security guards or warden. Maybe, they were not required in this notorious place. The boys were daring enough to secure themselves. If Uttar Pradesh (UP) was a country, it would have the smallest constitution ever written; "*Kayde main rahogey, faydey main rahogey*". This line tells the complete story of UP, as the notorious six-word story of Hemmingway does.

Sunil noticed two boys silhouetted through the first-floor balcony when entering the courtyard in the dim flickering light. One was short and stout in a white *baniyaan*, and the other guy was wearing a net-vest that showed his nipples. The sight of the hairy dark nipple irked Sunil.

"Don't worry, you are with me. They cannot harm you," said Guddu when he sensed the fear in Sunil.

Guddu gazed back, and they scurried back inside their room.

"The short one is Vinod Yadav, and the other is Rajiv Mahto. They all are too old to be called university students. They have been flunking deliberately to be in politics." said Uma.

"Don't make fun of anyone's age. I'm an old guy too. Twenty three. I'm doing M.Sc just to stay away from my home." Guddu turned towards Sunil, "That guy, Rajiv, he likes guys like you Sunil, a good-looking one, clean-shaven. But as you are a little stronger and taller than him, he may stay away from you," Guddu laughed.

"What do you mean?" asked Sunil.

"Nothing, you will get it eventually," Uma smirked.

"So, where are you from?" Guddu inquired further. Guddu was aware that Sunil and Uma knew each other, but was not sure how.

"I grew up in Delhi, but originally I'm from Meerut."

"*Bhaiya*, my *mamaji* who lives in Meerut and Sunil were neighbours. Sunil will shift to the hostel next month," said Uma.

"Where do you live here, Sunil?" Guddu asked. In the late midnight silence, Guddu noticed Sunil's baritone voice for the first time. It felt like he could see each word uttered like a drop of honey in water.

"*Bhaiya*, I'm staying with my relatives temporarily, near Barra, Shayam Nagar."

"Barra, isn't it the place of beauty number three?" Guddu sneered and looked at Uma.

Uma had two mental codexes: of all beautiful girls of Kanpur, ranked by himself; and the other, a list of all lovers mapped with the girls of list one. He had knowledge of each attribute, such as age, address, likes, dislikes, and what kind of guys they preferred.

"Yes, her name is Tunni. Beauty queen number three. You can say, Miss Asia Pacific of Kanpur."

"Who are the first two?" asked Sunil.

"Are you joking?" Uma looked at Sunil with amazement while climbing the stairs. "We just now tried to get a glimpse of the first one – Rimjhim, of course – and the second is Rakshita."

Guddu unlocked the door to room number 21. They entered the room. It was spacious, with a kitchen and a balcony.

"Do students here get such big rooms?"

"No, it was a staff room. *Bhaiya* liked it, and the university arranged it for *Bhaiya*," Uma said proudly.

"Forget about the room. I will try to get a nice one for you – not as big as this, but a corner room with a window. Until then go, play cricket in Barra. There is a *maidaan*, and kids play cricket there," said Guddu.

"Yeah, most of the boys there play cricket behind Tunni's house to get a sight of her. But beware, she is Bhujang's girl.

He is not dangerous, but he has Bechu Mishra's backup," Uma unfurled his knowledge.

"Bechu Mishra?"

"Yes, he is a goon from Barra, but don't worry. For the past few years, he has been busy shaping his career. Probably twenty-one years old, and he has completed his B.Com. He is a CA aspirant." said Uma.

"I have heard his name too but never met him," Guddu said. He drew more bottles of beer from a small fridge.

"I haven't seen him either, but I have heard that if outsiders try to tease a girl from Barra, he beats them black and blue. He is a saviour," Uma muttered.

"Ignore him. Go Sunil, enjoy Kanpur, eat *badnaam kulfi*, play cricket, take *panga* with a kid like Bechu Mishra. There is Guddu's Shukla hand on your head," Guddu smirked.

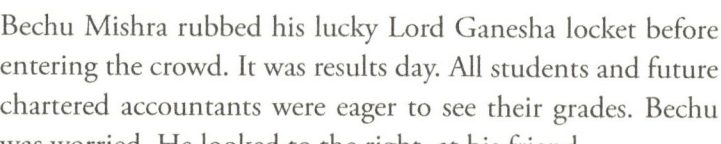

Bechu Mishra rubbed his lucky Lord Ganesha locket before entering the crowd. It was results day. All students and future chartered accountants were eager to see their grades. Bechu was worried. He looked to the right, at his friend.

Rishabh was listening to a Walkman. He pulled his Che Guevara printed t-shirt up and wiped the sweat off his forehead.

"If I don't pass this exam today, I'm gone," Bechu said.

"Pray to god and let's see the result," Rishabh said, in a light south Delhi Punjabi accent.

"You go first. We prepared together. If you pass, I will pass too."

Rishabh Khanna slipped through the student crowd until he reached the notice board, and hovered his finger above the alphabetically arranged names and roll codes. Rishabh found the most horrible word in the universe: FAIL. He grew disappointed and came out.

Bechu understood his body language; loose, bleak, his shoulders were down and lumpy, it narrated the whole story.

"What happened?" Bechu asked. He glanced towards Rishabh for a gesture of hope.

"This subject, accounts, is a real bitch!" Rishabh sighed.

It was Bechu's turn. He knew his fate. He struggled through the crowd, abusing some students. He crossed his fingers for good luck, touched his locket again and looked at the board after taking a deep breath.

After a few minutes, he came out of the crowd, smiling.

"What happened?" Rishabh jumped up. "Did you clear the exam? Great, you are a CA now." He forgot his own result for a moment.

"Accountancy is a real bitch!" Bechu smiled at him.

"What?"

"I agree, this subject is a bitch. It's biting, nipping, and shelving both of us."

"I don't get you?"

"Remember, we studied together, so we are bombed together."

Rishabh hugged Bechu. Now his happiness was more expansive than before.

They saw a young girl in blue jeans and a pink top running out of the crowd. Her low-pitched voice pierced everyone's ear. "I topped in accounts," she declared.

Annoyed, Bechu looked at Rishabh. "How come this beauty queen cleared the exam? What do they do?" Bechu asked.

"Ignore her. You know they mug everything. These girls, they don't have real knowledge," Rishabh said.

"Even of Accounts?"

They laughed loudly with amazement. The girl looked at them and ignored them, and got busy celebrating her success with other girls.

Disappointed and with slow strides, Bechu and Rishabh walked away from the Institute building. Both athletic and the same height – 5'7" – they also shared the same fate.

"Do you want to drink? We need to," Bechu said.

"Yes, but how we will get it?"

"Leave it up to me. I will ask Bhujang to bring it."

✳

Bhujang, a six-foot-tall, muscular guy, was famous in Kanpur. Not for his bravery or brain, but his dedicated passion for bodybuilding. He was also known for his commitment to his unrequited love, Tunni. Bhujang had a habit of licking his lips like a snake. Noticing this early, the colony boys named him Bhujang, meaning snake. Bhujang's real name, Abhyananda Yadav, got lost somewhere on his mark-sheet or in his birth certificate. No one called him Abhyananad afterwards.

After matriculation from UP board in Hindi medium, he had decided not to study further, as his goal was to open a gym. He was aware of all body muscles, diet plans and exercises needed to grow them. That was enough.

Bhujang looked at Bechu's house in the twilight. He squinted at the "to-let" sign put up by his father. He made a slight hissing sound and whispered, "*Bechu Bhaiya, Bechu Bhaiya.*" He was holding a crate of beers. While waiting, he pumped it, up and down, as if the container was a dumbbell.

"You will get me killed, *ek din tum bapu se marawaayega be,*" Bechu muttered. He and Rishabh came running down the stairs and pulled Bhujang aside. Bechu looked in every corner, ensuring no one was looking at him.

He slowly pulled out a rusted key and opened a lock on the ground floor.

They entered a dusty apartment. After jumping broken furniture, Bechu, Rishabh, and Bhujang moved to a corner room.

Bhujang gawked at the semi-nude pictures of models, cut from the *Times of India*'s third page, and the *Kanpur Times*. Bechu pulled the CA exam preparation books aside and placed the beer bottles down.

"You should not rent this unit. This is our den. An *adda*," Bhujang said while looking at Pamela Anderson's picture on the wall. He sank on the torn mattress.

"This apartment is my father's. It's his wish whenever he wants to put it up for rent or open a warehouse. I don't interfere with his business," Bechu said.

"But eventually, it's going to be yours."

"I don't care."

Rishabh opened beer bottles and spread some snacks on a newspaper: Bikaji *namkeen,* moong-daal mixtures, and masala peanuts.

Bhujang pulled out a packet of puffed rice, onion, and *dhaniya*. He chopped it using a knife and mixed it with mustard oil. A pungent smell of mustard oil penetrated their nostrils and watered their mouth when mixed with puffed rice.

"You have come with all the weapons of your arsenal," Bechu grinned.

"If you drink, drink royally," Bhujang winked.

Rishabh picked up one more bottle, opened the cap and offered the bottle to Bhujang.

Bhujang looked scornfully at him. He did not take the bottle from his hand. He picked one from the lot and popped its crowned cap using his *kada*. Rishabh ignored him.

"I love the smell of Kingfisher. By the way, what's the occasion?" Bhujang turned towards Bechu.

"We flunked, so we are celebrating. And yes, a Kingfisher is always great. You can drink it on all occasions. With it, you can celebrate birthdays, or you can mourn deaths," Bechu said.

He tossed some peanuts into his mouth.

"Oh, in that case, I will keep praying to God. He should flunk you every year," Bhujang said.

Bhujang poured beer in a plastic tumbler and took a swig. He burped, looked at Rishabh with hateful eyes and rolled an empty beer bottle on the floor.

"You educated people don't hang out with me nowadays," Bhujang said to Bechu.

"Bhujang, stop this comparison. Please don't start it again. We are all friends. I just don't get time because of all this CA stuff."

"*Bechu Bhaiya*, have you heard that song '*Jhoom Barabar jhoom sharabi*,' that quwali?" Bhujang asked to change the topic. He took the cassette from his pocket and inserted it into a cassette player.

"Keep the volume low. Chotu may hear," Rishabh said.

"*Abeey, saale angrez.* You don't talk. This is better than your English songs." He looked at Bechu, "What was that song? Show me the meaning of something! A girly song," Bhujang laughed.

Rishabh ignored Bhujang. He asked Bechu. "Then what's your next plan?"

"Not sure. It looks like I have to work at my father's shop," Bechu said.

Bhujang chugged the beer and picked a new bottle.

"I don't want to study further. I don't get it. I will open my gym." Bhujang massaged his forehead using his muscular fingers and rolled his eyes. "I think I'm down. I'm feeling tipsy," he declared and crashed on the pillow.

"I don't want to sit in my father's shop. I will take one more chance. I want to be a CA." Bechu, who was still on his first bottle, peeled the bottle's label using his thumbnail. He scraped as if he was trying to change his destiny… his skin. A sense of guilt crept into him.

"We've been flunking for the past three years, but still, I have hope. I missed it by a couple of marks," Rishabh said.

"How can you be so optimistic?" Bechu asked.

"Do you know Goran Ivanisevic?"

"That tennis player?"

"Yes, he lost the Wimbledon final against Agassi in 1992. Then again to Pete Sampras in 1995 and 1998. He had lost all hope. He was struggling with injury and motivation. Two years ago, in 2001, he had a wild card entry. His world ranking was 125 or something. But he won the final. Next year is going to be our wild card, Bechu. If he can win on the brink of retirement, why can't we? Let's embark on an unforgettable run like him."

Bechu was quiet for a moment. Rishabh's motivational and positive attitude always helped him to focus and take a decisive route. Bechu was aware that his father had given him many chances. But why should his father provide the chance? It was his life, and he should have the liberty to take as many chances as he wanted.

Fidgeting with the bottle in his hand, he looked at Bhujang, at how clear he was with his life. Bhujang never let his father control his choices.

Bechu noticed Bhujang was still holding his spinning head.

Bhujang looked at Rishabh and tried to say something, but crashed on the pillow. He reached out at the cassette player and switched it off with his fumbling hand. The *Qawwali* and Rishabh's talks were screeching in his head.

"I would advise you to talk to your dad once," Rishabh said. "He may give you one more chance."

"Dad, huh!" Bhujang smirked.

"Now, what happened?" Rishabh erupted. He had taken enough tantrums from him.

"The British are gone, but they left their illegitimate child behind. Who uses the word 'Dad' in Kanpur? Can't you use *Babuji*? Your father is dead, so everyone's fathers are dead?" Bhujang said.

"Bhujang, shut up!" Bechu screamed.

"Why are you taking the side of this jinx? He has killed many, including his father," Bhujang snarled.

Rishabh did not speak. He stared at the floor and drew his fist, but finally succeeded in controlling his anger. He got up and walked out. It was better he left, he thought. His father had drowned in a lake while saving Rishabh when he was eight years old. It was not Rishabh's mistake. Accidents happen.

"Rishabh, wait. He is drunk," Bechu ran after him and he saw the light of the sunset fade on the wall.

Joginder Mishra's usual daily activities included talking to retail business people and updating the accounts book. These were his mundane, boring routines that he performed with pride. He was remarking returned and damaged packages into his inventory book when he saw a bald man, who was gazing at the Jockey lady's undergarment advertisement. Joginder ripped the poster.

"This is for advertisement, not for your entertainment." He glared at the bald man.

Fazal Ganj, Kanpur's business hub, was always crowded. Joginder Mishra had made his place and had acquired the business of all undergarment's franchisees, from Rupa to Dora to Jockey. Joginder had a proud sense that the whole of Kanpur wrapped their bottoms in the cloth, *chaddi*, that passed through his massive wholesale shop.

Joginder Mishra was confused about life. Being a brahmin, he had taken an oath during his *upnayaan sanskar*, a threading ceremony, that he would not touch *madira*. He wore that thread dutifully, except for thirty minutes at night.

Every night at 10:00 pm, he would make himself two pegs. He would attribute the alcohol droplets to *ishan, aagneya, vayvya* and *neshrta* directions. He would then remove his *janeva* thread for precisely thirty minutes. He would complete his pegs and then put the thread back on at exactly 10:30 pm. This was his daily routine.

During these thirty minutes, he also would make sure that he watched his favourite show. The whole day, Joginder Mishra, who could give hours of lectures on Indian *sanskriti*, *sabhyata* and culture, could take a flip at 10:00 pm. He played MTV every night, and his favourite show was *The Grind*. In those thirty minutes, he committed all his sins for the day.

Joginder Mishra was a confused father, and he was an unbalanced mixture of Amrish Puri and Anupam Kher. By nature, he was Amrish Puri, but he had shown his Anupam Kher side of fatherhood once.

His son, Bechu Mishra, had passed with average marks in his board exams. Bechu had to select his choice of subject, either science or commerce. Arts has no place in a middle-class family.

Like uncommon tradition in North India, Uttar Pradesh, Bechu showed his rebellious side and opted for commerce. Bechu, with little hesitation, had rebelled and announced, "I want to do B.Com. and will become a CA." That day, Bechu's extended family was so quiet you could have heard a soap bubble pop. Bechu's Chachi had declared that Bechu was weak in maths, so he could not pursue science without knowing that accountancy is maths.

Joginder Mishra was impressed by the movie *DDLJ* and he had that hangover for five years. Joginder approved his son's decision, and after two weeks, he repented when one of his uninformed opinionated friends had mentioned that CA is not as good as engineering.

But Joginder was Joginder. He never expressed his emotion to his son. Once a decision was made, it was made. He was committed to it. His son would become a CA – even though he had no clue what a CA did.

But after a few weeks, he was back from Anupam to Amrish mode. Whenever anyone from his colony completed IIT or AIIM, Joginder would have an extra glass of Old Monk, his favourite rum. Bechu used to gauge his father's happiness based on the number of drinks he had consumed. One drink, Joginder was a happy man; two glasses, Joginder was sad. Three meant he was depressed.

Today, Joginder was ready for an extra glass. He returned from his shop at exactly seven and retrieved the new bottle from his little bar in the corner of the drawing-room. Bechu was in his room. He had played the dining room scene thrice. The result-talk would always happen at the dining table, at 8:00 pm sharp. For the past three years, the talk on result day had been the same: *nahi hota then kuch aur kyun nahi kar lete, try UPSC.* His father never used to talk before and after dinner.

At 8:00 pm, Bechu's mother served dinner. Bechu came to the table with an absent and uninterested mind. He picked at a pickle and a few rotis.

Today even the tinkle of cutlery on plates sounded loud in the silence. Unaware of the matter's sensitivity, Chotu, Bechu's younger brother, turned on the TV. He switched the channel to Cartoon Network. Joginder stared at his wife with his big eyes, and she switched off the TV.

"Sit down and have your dinner," Mother commanded Chotu. She was aware that her voice was not important, like her name. In patriarchy, wives adopt their husband's name, and even the thoughts are not their own – the husband's opinion rules.

The silence in the house had made it very clear what the result was. Joginder did not ask, but he knew the answer.

"So, what's next? You're getting older. Have you thought about it?" Joginder asked, forcing himself to remain calm.

Bechu did not speak and pushed a morsel of *roti* into his mouth. His father's words were strangling him. This is how failure crushes you: every second tastes sour, and every moment stinks.

"Last year I advised you, if you cannot pass the CA exam, try Railway, Bank or something else. Now I know you are not smart enough for UPSC. But you can try other competitive exams."

Bechu was staring at the salt and pepper shakers in front of him. He picked the salt up absentmindedly but was unaware of where to put more salt. He fidgeted with it for a few seconds, then returned it to the table. All he could hear was the sound of the ceiling fan.

"From next month, you can come and help me. I have established a business, and I need some accountancy help," his father declared.

"I don't want to sell *chaddi*," Bechu erupted.

"Do the educated people talk like this? A business is a business," Joginder shouted. "Learn from Chotu. He is mature. He knows how to respect his father. Check his results. He tops his classes. Learn something from him."

"Chotu is in the third grade, and I'm doing CA. Don't you understand the difference?" Bechu slid down in his chair and pounded the table with frustration.

"Are you arguing with your father? Is this what they teach you in your CA curriculum? Was it for a day like this that I approved your decision to study B.Com?" Joginder asked, infuriated.

Bechu pushed back his chair and rose to return to his room. The chair fell to the floor with a loud thud. A few tears fell from Chotu's eyes, and his mother told him to go to his room. Chotu was confused about what to do now to placate the situation. He went to the bathroom and started brushing his teeth. He never used to brush in the evening.

Chotu came back to the dining room holding a toothbrush. Joginder looked at Bechu's mother with confused eyes.

"Chotu, go to your room," his mother requested.

Chotu immediately followed her instruction.

It was ten at night. Joginder opened his brand-new bottle of Old Monk and poured himself a peg. He was worried about his son's future but wanted to release all his stress for the next thirty minutes. After the first drink, the DDLJ's Anupam mode was on.

Instead of talking directly to his son and motivating him, he commanded his wife to do so. Indian middle-class fathers are always clueless about how to deal with situations such as this. Running away from real talk or mistreating their wives to vent their stress is usually their solution.

"Tell him that he can try again. From next year, he can help me. My business can be his backup plan." He did not make direct eye contact with his wife and searched for the MTV channel on TV. A few bikini-clad models danced on the screen.

Frustrated, Bechu tore his last year's notebooks. Today he felt like his home was becoming a jail. But then, he remembered about Goran Ivanisevic. He took a piece of paper, wrote "Mission: CA final" on it, and underlined it. He rearranged his books. He was ready for his wild card entry.

✳

Bechu's mother, Sumati Devi, arranged a variety of snacks on a plate. It was a familiar ritual among all the middle-class families across the country. Snacks and quality biscuits are always for guests. Eight-year-old Chotu was one of the victims. He loathed the bulky guest who had a curly shoe-brush moustache in his drawing-room. It was Shatrughan Singh. Chotu stared at the biscuit plate and prayed that they wouldn't eat them all.

"Rent in Kanpur is minuscule. We have done business together, pay according to the market. You are a contractor. You know it better. I look for a good family," Joginder said.

"*Mishra Ji*, don't worry about anything. We will treat your house as if it were our own," Shatrughan said.

Chotu looked at Shatrughan Singh. He hovered around for the cream biscuit, waiting for Shatrughan to depart.

"No, please don't. The last tenant, Sharma Ji, stayed for ten years, and we did not even increase the rent once. He also considered the house his own. Last year, Papa had to call in some goons to get rid of him," said Chotu. His mouth watered as he watched Shatrughan crack a biscuit and savour it.

Shatrughan Singh frowned at Chotu, he was frustrated, but could not show his anger. He had to find a new house.

Joginder Mishra eyed Chotu knowingly. Aware of the situation, Bechu's mother came forward to lighten the mood. "*Chal bhaag yahan se*, he has become naughty," she smiled. "New generation kids, they don't know how to behave in front of their elders. Cable TV is ruining them," she declared. She noticed Choutu's greedy eyes and gave him a severe look of warning.

"I have a small family of four: my wife, myself and two daughters, Rimjhim and Rakshita." Shatrughan's fingers reached out for the last biscuit, but Chotu snatched it and ran away. Stunned and embarrassed, Shatrughan smirked and picked up the cup of tea.

"You need to control him," Joginder screamed.

"It's fine. They're all naughty at this age. Perhaps you could just show me the apartment?"

"We need to get the unit cleaned— our eldest son Bechu uses it for his exam prep. Come next week and we'll show you. But it's the same as this unit. We stay on the first floor, and the ground floor will be yours. It's almost the same. You can see our house, and there is no difference."

Shatrughan had made a mistake. He had used his rifle in public, and his current landlord had given him an ultimatum to vacate. Waiting for a week would have been a disaster. Many house owners were not ready to share their house on rent to a contractor. On top of that, in Kanpur, if your daughter was young and beautiful, your alley would be full of stalkers. People were aware of this – everyone except Joginder Mishra. Shatrughan Singh wanted to close the deal as soon as possible.

"No, no. No need to see it then. It's beautiful. Here is a month's advance rent. Five thousand rupees a month," Shatrughan offered.

The rental offer was less, and Joginder was aware of this. He never had a retail business mindset. He was in the wholesale business, and negotiating for a few hundred rupees was beneath his pride. Without counting the notes, he gave it to his wife. He felt the urge to brag about his family tradition to Shatrughan. "I never count money, *Singh sahib*. None of my great grandfathers or forefathers counted *chillars*. Once my grandfather went to a village, to talk about his daughter's marriage. While discussing the proposal, a servant came and returned the money to his master, a few *annas*. That miser counted the money in front of the servant as well as my grandfather. My grandfather did not marry my *Bua* to that house. He just got up and folded his hands and walked out." Joginder's eyes gleamed with pride.

Shatrughan listened carefully. He could not tell whether Joginder was bragging or insulting Shatrughan.

"Nice. I will come next week and take the keys. I will shift this month-end," Shatrughan said.

✳

Cricket is the perfect getaway when you are stressed. A new guy, Sunil Chauhan, was a sensation, and Bechu had heard he was quick.

"He must be as fast as Zaheer Khan," Bhujang said to Bechu when Bechu took guard.

Sunil stood at the beginning of his long run-up, rubbing a tennis ball near his crotch.

"*Abye behanchod*, bowlers do this to keep the shine of the leather ball. This is a tennis ball." Bechu screamed at Sunil.

Sunil ignored him. His muscular legs propelled him through his long run-up. Bechu took his stance, but the ball hit the wickets directly.

"First, learn how to play before commenting on others," said Sunil, and he gave an outraged look to Bechu.

All the guys in the field were too scared to say a word. Sunil, new to the colony, noticed this silence, but he dared. He analysed the situation and mellowed his tone. "Bechu, you are out," Sunil Chauhan said reluctantly.

"This was warm-up. I was not ready," Bechu said. "And I'm not Bechu to you. Show some respect and say *Bechu Bhaiya*," Bechu said to Sunil, looking directly into his eyes.

"A warm-up ball in the middle of the game?" Sunil asked, collecting his confidence, but his adam's apple quivered.

"Mr *Zhandu balm*, don't try to be a hero. In this colony, *Bechu Bhaiya* is the one and only superman. *Ek kantaap dengey aur puri rangbaazi jhad dengey*. Go bowl." Bhujang frowned from his stance as wicket-keeper.

Sunil bowled again. Bechu hit a few shots. Sunil got tired after a few overs and bowled a few wides.

"Can someone else bowl? This guy is no good," Bechu shouted, and a new guy took the ball.

Sunil wiped his sweat and went to the boundary. He was furious, and his face was radiating anger. He noticed that a guy in a fancy Bob Marley t-shirt was scribbling something in a notebook.

"What are you writing?" Sunil asked.

"Just a poem. New to this colony and the city?" the guy replied. His name was Rishabh Khanna.

"Yes." Sunil looked around. He was tired and irritated that he had been bullied by Bechu for no reason.

"So here, people always play one-sided cricket?" Sunil asked.

"Not one-sided. It's Bechu-sided." Rishabh laughed. "He is the *Bhaiya* of this colony, the respected one, you know. But don't worry, from tomorrow he will not come to the ground. You can play your game. Today, he is frustrated."

"What an asshole, and what a weird name. Who names their son Bechu?"

"His name is Amit Mishra, Bechu is his nickname."

"What do you do apart from writing this poetry?

"I'm Bechu's good friend. We are both CA candidates. I write in my free time, want to read?"

"Oh, sorry to insult your friend, but yes, I would like to."
Sunil bit his tongue. "Don't talk about this to Bechu, please,
that I called him an asshole," he continued.

"Don't worry, he is a nice guy, and I will zip my mouth."

"Who is that muscular guy? He is a loudmouth. I will not
spare him," Sunil growled. "Your accent says that you are not
from Kanpur."

"I don't care what you have perceived," said Rishabh.

"I have perceived that this bulky guy is very foul-mouthed.
I'm new to this area. If this was Meerut, I would have taught
him a lesson," Sunil said.

When Sunil roved his eyes to nearby houses, he saw a girl
come to a terrace. She was petite and dusky, and Bhunjag
gawked at her. Sunil followed the direction in which Bhujang
was casting his amorous eyes.

"This girl must be Tunni," Sunil said.

"Yes. How do you know?"

"I had my orientation class about Kanpur. A few college
friends mentioned her."

"Oh, I was not aware she is that famous," Rishabh laughed.
"This guy Bhujang likes her a lot. Half of the guys playing
here come just to get a glimpse of Tunni. But now I know she
is famous in Meerut too," Rishabh said.

Tunni took a towel and brushed it through her silky hair.
Many guys on the field became mesmerized. Sunil looked at
her and took a deep breath.

"So even Bechu is in the queue for her?" Sunil asked.

"No, Cupid or Kaamdev has not built an arrow yet,
which can pierce the heart of Bechu," Rishabh said proudly.
"Beware of Bhujang and stay away from this girl. He likes
her," Rishabh warned.

"What if I fall in love with this girl?" Sunil asked.

"If you commit this folly, you will be accosted by him and given a black eye and a bruised cheek. He will grind your muscles using his dumbbells." Rishabh smiled. "But first, lover boy, if you have already taken a fancy for her then can you see those two vendors? One is selling *chaat* and *samosa*, and the other one at the book shop, just across from Tunni's house. Try to deal with them, then you can reach Bhujang."

Meanwhile, Chotu came running to the ground. He was faster than a Diwali rocket.

"*Bechu Bhaiya, labhed ho gaya*, we are in trouble. Papa has rented the house and asked you to clean the apartment," Chotu said.

"Oh man, when?" Bechu threw his bat and ran. He looked at Bhujang for help, but he was busy gawking at Tunni, who was enjoying the attention from the guys.

"Rishabh, come fast. We need to clean up," Bechu screamed.

Rishabh closed his diary and dusted down his pants. He smiled at Sunil. "See you soon, but beware, and I would recommend ignoring Bhujang."

✳

Bechu opened the lock. Rishabh and Chotu entered the apartment. Chotu was carrying big black plastic garbage bags.

"We should clean the house first, before his dad, ahh, the father comes," Rishabh said.

"You can use the word 'dad' in front of me. First, close Chotu's eyes."

Rishabh saw that Chotu was already in the room, gaping at the wall full of semi-nude pictures of Pamela Anderson and Salma Hayek. Chotu was amazed.

Rishabh smiled and covered Chotu's eyes with his hand. Chotu tried to remove it, but Rishabh's grip was tight. Chotu struggled.

"Let me see, I'm a big boy now. I'm also getting hair on my private parts."

"Just shut up," Bechu warned. He picked up the beer bottles and cigarette packets that they had left the previous night.

"Let me see, just a small glimpse, or else I will tell our father about the cigarettes," Chotu said.

"Don't blackmail us. Call me *Bhaiya*, and I will give you a sneak peek," Rishabh said.

"*Bhaiya*, please."

Rishabh revealed to him all the posters. Later, he peeled them off one by one, and Bechu collected them in garbage bags. They swept the floor and collected all the books in a box. Chotu looked at the plastic bag. The semi-nude Pamela was trying to escape, looking for a saviour. Chotu picked it up.

Sunil Chauhan, raised in Delhi but born in Meerut, was not an ordinary guy. He had seen the whole of Uttar Pradesh due to his father's job in banking, which had resulted in many transfers. Sunil had enough experience to have had a tussle with different types of boys. He knew how to take revenge and settle a score. And the best way to settle a score with Bhujang was to snatch his girl. About Bechu, he would think later.

Sunil had noticed that Tunni was trying to get attention, but all the guys were scared. They were missing the crucial part. They were not taking the first and the boldest step. In the war of attraction, the first step matters. Girls select their partners on the basis of this first act of bravery. The first step is the sign of courage.

Sunil reached the magazine shop to test the water, which was just across from Tunni's house. In a small colony, everyone knows the new guy. Outsiders are always blue-eyed boys in middle-class colonies. Sunil was aware of this fact. He cashed in on it.

Sunil asked the vendor about English magazines and started flipping through them. As anticipated, at 5:00 pm, Tunni came to the terrace. Other lover boys, like Bhujang, were on the cricket field, but Sunil was on the field of the real game. He was batting for revenge.

Sunil was just looking for eye contact. He wore his sunglasses. Tunni, as was her habit, scanned the whole field and the street across from her house. She gauged how many were looking at her. She always liked this attention.

She looked at the tall guy in rugged white jeans, parted hair, and a dark blue t-shirt. The guy removed his sunglasses to get a better peek. That guy was Sunil. She knew about him.

Sunil timed the eye contact. He held Tunni's gaze for a few seconds and then turned towards the magazine shop. He knew the game of attraction. He knew how to make girls curious.

After a few minutes, Tunni opened her gate and crossed the road in the light traffic of Barra Bazar. The *chaat* vendor, Afzal, turned toward the *magazine-wala* with excitement. "Today she will come to my shop," he gushed, and he combed his hair twice. Afzal looked at the mirror which he had placed next to his *Golgappa* counter. He combed his hair some more.

"First check your a*ukaat*, your stature. You're only five feet tall, and she is five foot two. Second, her father is a lawyer, and you are selling *chat-samosa*," the magazine vendor, Gupta, declared. He applied Fair & Lovely to his face and smelled his palm.

"So what, have you seen the movie *Raja Hindustani*? The mere taxi driver, Amir Khan, impressed the girl and wooed her. You just need a pure heart and true love," Afzal said.

"But that guy was Amir Khan. Look at your face," Gupta said.

While listening to this, Sunil laughed.

"*Bhai Saab*, am I wrong?" Gupta asked Sunil. Meanwhile, Gupta noticed that Tunni was two feet away from the *chat* shop and ten feet from his. Nervously, Gupta sniffed his armpit, the last check to be presentable in front of Kanpur beauty.

Tunni looked at Sunil. She played with her hair and asked Afzal, "*Bhaiya*, one plate *paani ke batase*, and make it a parcel." She again looked at Sunil, made eye contact and smiled.

Gupta first grinned and then giggled when he heard the word "*Bhaiya*" for Afzal. *Paani-puri, golgappa, phuchka* are the names of the same Indian exquisite street food delicacy which unites India through taste. And when Afzal cracked the puri with his thumb to prepare Tunni's parcel his heart crumbled. He was a Muslim, it should be fine to get called 'bhaiya' but he knew he was now 'Bhai-zoned' which was the next level of getting friend-zoned.

Knowing the game, Sunil looked directly into her eyes, gave her a half-smile, and turned towards the vendor. If you want a girl's attention, ignore her first. He used his husky baritone voice and asked in English, "Show me that new issue of *Cineblitz*."

Tunni walked past the *chaat* shop and stood next to Sunil. She picked up the magazine Sunil was reading and brushed her hand against his. "I have already read this issue," she said and looked into his eyes. She smiled and turned back.

She took the parcel, crossed the road and walked towards her door. This time she intentionally did not turn back. She had seen the movie *DDLJ*, and turning meant giving a hint. She wanted this attraction game alive in Sunil's heart.

The *chaat* vendor and *magazine-wala* were stunned. Sunil started his bike, revved his engine, and drove away doing a little wheely stunt. The vroom sound gave Tunni goosebumps.

This new guy of the colony had impressed her in seconds when all the other guys had been trying for years.

✳

Rishabh's Swaroop Nagar apartment was like any modern apartment which was bubbling in India. It was equipped with security features, party halls and a gymnasium.

The teapot came to a boil, steaming and whistling. Rishabh poured tea into a porcelain cup and handed it to Bechu. Bechu looked at the poster of Freddie Mercury, a depiction of his Live Aid concert. Rishabh had told this story to Bechu many times. About Freddy's songs. Bechu had listened to "Bohemian Rhapsody" many times to write the lyrics in his diary. "Is this real life? Is this just fantasy?" Bechu never understood why Rishabh liked this sad song, but he knew he was sensitive.

"Sorry for that day… Bhujang misbehaved with you," Bechu said. He sipped the tea. He always liked the mild ginger flavour. Rishabh knew the exact quantity of ginger a cup of tea should have.

"Which day?" Rishabh asked.

"That 'dead dad' remark."

"Oh! Then why are you sorry? It's Bhujang, he should be sorry for this." Rishabh put in the cassette of Bohemian Rhapsody. Bechu felt that Rishabh could read his mind. He always liked this about Rishabh.

"Don't feel bad. I know you tolerate him because of me. I'm not sure why he does not like you. Please ignore him… for me…" Bechu pleaded. Bechu noticed that Rishabh again looked out at the window and sighed. This silence always killed Bechu. He continued, "Look, you are different. You talk like a mature, knowledgeable person, like an English man. Everyone wants to be like you, so they are jealous. Look at you, you play the guitar, you hum English songs. Do you know girls used to be crazy about you in our CA institute tuition classes?"

"Let's forget it." Rishabh looked at Bechu and smiled forcibly. "You are my friend, and that's enough for me."

Bechu hugged him. He liked the cologne that Rishabh was wearing, Bechu smiled. He remembered why Bhujang called him a *ladki*, a girl. According to Bhujang, a guy wearing cologne or perfume was a sign of female quality.

"You know, I have a dream that after completing the CA exam, we shall open a firm, which we shall name 'Mishra and Khanna associates.'"

"Let's clear the exam first, my dear friend. Did you speak to your father?" Rishabh asked. He avoided repeating the word 'dad'.

"Yes, and I'm going to start with tax law this time. Come to my house tomorrow. We will go to Parade Ground and buy some books," Bechu flipped an issue of *Sportstar* magazine. He saw an article on Goran Ivanisevic. "Oh, so this was the source of your preachy speech?" Bechu noticed that Rishabh smiled after a long time.

✳

It was the month of June and sweat trickled down Bechu's spine. His father had allowed Bechu to take his bike to the Parade Ground, but the first condition was to clean the bike. It was eleven in the morning, but the sun was scorching hot.

"Pass me that blue bucket," Bechu said to Rishabh.

"I think we can go first, get books and should clean this in the evening," Rishabh said.

"You don't know my dad. He is an Amrish Puri. After Parade Ground, we are going to his shop, we will drop this bike there and take an auto back home!"

After a few minutes of cleaning, they saw a young lad approach on an Rx100 bike. His bike had a Chunky Pandey sticker, and he was wearing sunglasses and a shirt with a bold sunflower print. He parked his bike in front of Bechu's house and opened the iron gate with confidence. He scanned the front yard and looked at Rishabh.

"Hello, you must be *Bechu Bhaiya*. I am Uma Nath Pandey, district topper for the whole of Kanpur for the year '99. These days, I have been preparing for IIT-JEE," Uma grinned. He stretched out his hands to Rishabh to shake it.

"*Introduction de raha hai ya apna resume padh raha hai,*" Bechu said. He placed the mop on the floor.

"What?" Uma said.

"Bechu Mishra is there," Rishabh pointed Uma in the right direction. Bechu was staring at him.

"Bechu sir, I am Uma Pandey, the 1999 district topper." Uma changed his stance. He picked up a rag and started dusting Bechu's bike.

"I've heard your introduction; now, can you stop and tell us what you need?" Bechu frowned. Bechu noticed that Uma was looking at the ground floor house, trying to get a peek of an open window. Bechu snatched the rag from Uma's hand.

"What's the matter? Why are you so happy and eager to help?" Bechu said.

"*Bhaiya*, you did not put this house up for rent yet?"

"If you are thinking of renting it, forget it. I don't rent to a Chunky Pandey like you. It's already been rented out – the tenants are moving in next week. From the look of you, I can say you are a cable TV operator. Never seen you in this colony?"

"No *Bhaiya*, I'm neither Chunky Pandey nor cable TV operator. I just wanted to recce this area," Uma said.

"Reece for what?" Rishabh asked.

"Oh *Bhaiya*, I have heard that Rakshita will come here to stay. So…," Uma said

"Who is Rakshita?" Bechu asked.

"Sister of Rimjhim."

"And, who is Rimjhim? Some skill of your resume?" Bechu laughed.

"*Bhaiya*, Rimjhim is a love interest of *Guddu Bhaiya*, you don't know him? The whole of Kanpur knows *Guddu Bhaiya* loves Rimjhim."

"*Abye oye jhandu*, you bloody stalker. You better cut the crap and get out of here, else I will give you a *kantaap*, a tight slap. Whole life, you will be like Chunky Pandey," Bechu broke out in anger.

"*Haan Bhaiya*, I'm going, but I have a humble request. Please don't fancy Rakhsita. Also, she might be four to five years younger than you. I have loved her from my childhood, unrequited love. We studied in the same high school, KV, Kendriya Vidyalaya. You can like Rimjhim. She is equally beautiful. I'm giving you freedom there."

"Shut the fuck up and get lost!" Bechu warned, and threw the blue bucket on him. Uma jumped on his Rx100 and drove away.

"Unrequited love. Are you serious! Who is this guy?" Rishabh asked.

"Let's ignore these *Majnus*. I don't want to focus on them. This year, focus on the CA final exam. My *bapu* has already given me an ultimatum. We are getting late. We need to buy books, give this bike to father and then stick with my study plans and schedule." Bechu kicked his bike.

✳

Bechu checked the clock. It was 4:30 in the evening. As planned, he had studied half of the direct tax laws topic. His brain was saturated, and he needed tea and rest.

It was time for his father, Joginder Mishra, to arrive. His arrival from the shop always dampened the mood at home. Television was not allowed after that. Bechu timed it with his other paper preparation, advanced management accounting. He had cleared the Final group 1 papers, two years ago, but his pace was like a snail after that. Tax laws were not his favourite subjects. He struggled with them: Central Excise, Service Tax, VAT and Customs, and Indirect taxes topics. He loathed them all.

Bechu looked at the next bed. Chotu had thrown his school bag on it. He took his books and arranged them on the shelves. Bechu had to share a room, like any siblings. He never liked Chotu's disorganized behaviour and wanted to shift him to the next room. There was another room in their four-bedroom apartment, but that was always empty. No one would ever go there. The door was always locked.

Bechu took some rest and walked down the stairs. He saw, in the paved front yard, that Chotu had placed a book on the wall. Chotu tossed a ball against the wall and hit it when it returned. He saw Bechu and smiled.

"Want to play with me?" Chotu asked.

"Yes, go bat, give me the ball. I will give you some batting practice."

Bechu bowled slowly. Right-handed Chotu played left-handedly. He tried to mimic Sourav Ganguly. He paused for a moment and looked at Bechu for validation.

"Great shot!" Bechu shouted. He knew Chotu would not move an inch until he praised him.

"Shhh, don't scream. Amrish Puri is here. In his room." Chotu signalled upstairs.

"What, how come?"

"Tenants are coming, that *motu,* that bulky fatso with the curly moustache, he is coming to get the keys."

"Oh, what is his name?"

"Shatrughan Singh. The name only sounds dangerous. He is a contractor."

"Oh, Amrish Puri has given our house to some *'Thakur'?*"

"Yes, Amrish Puri played Thakur in most of his movies, so our Amrish must be liking *Thakurs*! Now he has even given the apartment on rent to a *Thakur,*" Chotu said.

"But they eat non-veg food, and Amrish does not like it. He has hidden the Anupam Kher mode. Maybe that was active when renting the lower unit," said Bechu.

"No, I think Amrish is worried about money."

"Why?"

"He is not getting help from his elder son. His son is still studying instead of making some money. Amrish had to rent his house to some Rajput, even if they are going to cook meat in this holy place."

Bechu grabbed the collar of Chotu. "Don't taunt your elder brother. You've got to behave like a kid."

"I'm sorry, Bechu, if the harsh reality pierced your heart," Chotu continued.

"Will you stop?" Bechu barked.

✳

Meanwhile, they saw that a Jeep had arrived across the street. A bulky six-foot-tall man got down, accompanied by four henchmen. He walked with confidence, wearing a white *pyjama-kurta* with black *bandi*, and opened the gate.

"He is the *motu*, our new tenant. I was talking about him," Chotu whispered.

Shatrughan Singh looked at Bechu. He scanned and asked, "Are you the eldest son of *Mishra Ji*?"

"Yes."

"Can you call *Joginder babu*? Need to get the keys," Shatrughan said.

Finding the right opportunity, Chotu screamed, "Papa, Shatrughan Singh is here for the keys."

Joginder Mishra looked down from the first floor. He was in this typical home attire: a white *pyjama* and white full *ganji*, (vest).

"Oh, *Shatrughan Babu*, you are very punctual. Come up, have some snacks and tea," Joginder Mishra said.

"No, no, I just came for the keys. I will shift this weekend. So I thought I'll get the place cleaned and keep some token furniture. As a tradition, we will move the Ganesh Idol first." He looked back at his henchmen and gestured, "Some acquaintances are waiting for me."

Joginder Mishra looked across the street. Four henchmen were in the Jeep and staring at the house. They were looking like *Meghnad*, and other *Rakshasas*, standing beside *Ravana*. Bulky, dark, and tall. Uncomfortable, Joginder wiped the sweat from his forehead. "I will come down and give you the keys," he said, then disappeared.

Shatrughan realized that he had made another mistake. He had fired his rifle in his last colony, and his neighbours grew concerned. Now, he had brought some of his henchmen, and his new landlord looked worried. To dispel the awkwardness, he looked at Chotu. He thought about starting a conversation with him.

"Are you the youngest one?" Shatrughan asked.

"Yes, we have met once, and I'm not sure why you are asking again. I'm Chotu."

"Why did not you go upstairs and fetch the keys, instead of shouting to your father? Is this the *sanskaar* you are getting here in your family?" Shatrughan said.

Chotu ignored him. He turned back and took a stance for batting, but soon he realized that his father would come down. He would see him playing. Chotu threw the bat and picked up his book.

Bechu positioned himself and started teaching Chotu. Both brothers were so good at it. It looked like a natural act.

Within five minutes, Joginder Mishra came down. He handed over the key and looked again at Shatrughan's henchmen. Shatrughan anticipated his apprehension.

"Mishra ji, I'm a contractor. You know how notorious this business is. Sometimes I need them to run the business. I'm assuring you; I won't allow them to enter my house. Next time, you won't see them in this colony."

Joginder folded his hand and bid a namaste. He climbed back up the stairs. He did not say anything.

Shatrughan turned and looked at Bechu. He scanned him again, from top to bottom. If you are a father of two beautiful daughters in India, you treat every guy as a scallywag.

"Looks like you play every day. Do you study?" Shatrughan said.

"Yes."

"What is your background?"

"What do you mean?"

"I mean, IIT-JEE, medical, UPSC, what are you aiming for?" Shatrughan frowned.

"I've completed my B.Com., and I'm in CA final year."

"CA?" Shatrughan Singh made a face as if Bechu was a criminal.

"Chartered Accountancy."

"Why? You did not get admission for science?" Shatrughan gave a suspicious look to Bechu. He beckoned his henchmen to start the Jeep. He turned and opened the gate, and the rusty gate creaked.

Shatrughan was also rusty, like his old-fashioned opinions. Bechu threw his ball in anger and walked towards his room. He knew that the Kanpur society still respected IIT students. He had been good at science but started loathing it because of his science teacher in his high school, B.N. Lal. Bechu never liked him, so he never liked this subject. When he took commerce in his twelfth grade, his family and relatives were against him, but his father supported him. That was the last time he had seen his father's Anupam mode.

Bhujang took a shower and got ready. Today, he had decided that he would not go to the cricket ground but would stand in front of Tunni's house and look at her. He would appreciate her beauty. And if she would come to any of the shops across her house, he would try to talk to her.

He combed his hair twice. He thought of calling Bechu and getting some advice. But he knew Bechu was busy. Bechu had to clear his exam this time, and Bhujang wanted to support him. Bhujang applied deo, which he had seen in an advertisement. The Axe Effect: the ad showed that girls run behind a guy who used it. Bhujang wished that this would be his fate too. Tunni would take a sniff and get crazy about him. But he knew this happened only in ads.

Bhujang and Tunni studied in the same high school, Army Public School at Kanpur Cantonment. He was four years senior to Tunni. Bechu and Bhujang were classmates and were elder to all of the boys among Barra's Shyam Nagar colony.

Bhujang liked Tunni, his junior, from his school days but never had the courage to share his feelings.

This evening also, at the age of twenty-two, Bhujang was chickenhearted. He stood at Gupta's shop and made a hole in the newspaper. He searched for Tunni through it while faking that he was reading the newspaper. He looked at the terrace-balcony of the third floor. Tunni was not there. He waited. He looked at the magazine vendor. Gupta smiled. He never dared to say anything to Bhujang. He knew Bhujang was Bechu's friend.

Though the *magazine-wala*, Gupta, also liked Tunni, his business was more important than love and his competitor.

"*Bhujang Bhaiya*, do you know there is a new bee for this flower?" Gupta asked.

"What do you mean?"

"He means Sunil Chauhan. He is not even a bee, he is a wasp. You will keep peeping through this hole, and he will make a hole in your heart. He is handsome." Afzal put some fuel on the fire.

"That new guy who lives in 'Rajput house'?" Bhujang said.

"Yes, that proud man with a moustache is his uncle, and now Sunil has moved to the hostel, DAV, at Civil Lines. Now, he is part of the Guddu Shukla gang," Gupta said. "You know Guddu Shukla, right? Your muscles are nothing in front of his courage. And Tunni, she likes this guy. *Bhujang Bhaiya*, do something," Afzal said.

There was some movement on the terrace. Bhujang, Gupta and Afzal all went silent. Someone had come out to the balcony and it was probably Tunni.

Tunni emerged. She flipped her wet hair and spread the towel on a rope. Bhujang's heart fluttered like a pigeon. Afzal and Gupta were also smitten by her beauty. Within a few seconds, Tunni's mother, a beautiful woman in her mid-forties, came out and asked Tunni to go inside.

"Ahh, shit!" Afzal said.

Bhujang looked at him, "Why the hell are you feeling bad and groaning with disappointment?" he frowned.

Tunni went inside without noticing him, and it sank Bhujang's heart to his stomach.

"No *Bhujang Bhaiya*, there was a fly in the *papadi-chat*." Afzal pretended to drive some flies away, trying to mask his thought process from Bhujang. He was aware that if dolt Bhujang could even sniff his snide remark, he would smash him into pulp.

Gupta scowled at Afzal. Gupta, Afzal and Bhujang all harboured an unrequited love for Tunni, but Bhujang had been ahead of them until Sunil came and took the bold step of stealing Tunni's heart.

After five minutes, Sunil Chauhan came. He was on his Pulsar 500CC motorbike. He revved his bike when he entered the alley. Sunil's hair was neatly combed, and his shirt was well pressed without any wrinkles. He stopped his bike in front of Tunni's house. He checked his wristwatch, removed his leather biker's gloves, and pulled out a chit from his blue boot-cut jeans.

Tunni came back to the terrace again. She tucked her hair behind her ears and smiled at Sunil. She waved her hand to Sunil reluctantly, but looked across the street and pulled it back. This time she noticed Bhujang. She wanted to gesture to Sunil about him, but she did not.

Sunil was in his world. He wrapped a small piece of paper around a stone and threw it at the fourth floor. Tunni caught it like a cricketer. She had become a master while watching her admirers playing cricket behind her house. She opened it, and some rose petals flew in the wind. Tunni read:

Main chahta tha ki tum ko gulab pesh karun
Tum khud gulab ho tumko gulab kya deta.

Meet me at Ganga Ghat tomorrow at 5:00 pm after your chemistry tuition class. I will be waiting outside your tuition to pick you up.

Tunni smiled. This time she ignored the fear of Bhujang. Somehow, she felt that Sunil was the guy who could handle any of her stalkers. She looked back, cautious, as her mother was hovering around. She turned around and waved bye to Sunil without any hesitation, then blew a kiss in the air.

Bhujang witnessed this courage. He threw his newspaper and burned with anger. "*Madharchod*," he screamed.

Sunil tried twice to kick-start his bike. He had heard the adage that *purabiyas* are soft at heart and play dumb at love games, but they beat their opponents to a pulp when they are angry. He tried to kick-start his bike again, but had no luck. He put his bike on the stand and started running.

Bhujang chased. He turned and shouted at Afzal and Gupta, who were dumbstruck. "Are you going to chase that stupid-*chutiya*?"

Sunil pushed past a few hawkers and jumped handcarts. His heart was racing, and he had to save his life. He could hear Bhujang's heavy strides coming towards him. He had read about Doppler Effect in high school physics, but it was the first time he felt it himself. It was a live experiment. Seeing an auto, Sunil jumped inside.

"Just gun the engine and go, or else we both will be killed," Sunil shouted at the *auto-wala*. "*Abey labhed ho jayega*, let's get lost," Sunil used the Kanpuri dialect to persuade the *auto-wala*.

The *auto-wala* saw that a muscular guy and two of his sidekicks were running towards him. "Hey, he seems like

Bhujang, Bechu's man," the *auto-wala* said while revving his auto.

"Will you just speed up? Otherwise, we will see the dawn in the hospital," Sunil smacked at his head. The auto accelerated. In a side mirror, Sunil saw that Bhujang and his men's height decreased with distance and later disappeared in the Kanpur Street crowd.

Sunil took a deep breath and wiped his head. He had equalled his score with Bhujang, now it was Bechu's turn. Thinking about his plan for revenge, Sunil picked a comb from his side pocket and brushed his hair. He smiled and whistled softly. He liked the taste of his sweet revenge, and Tunni was a reward for his revenge plan. He would teach these *purabiyas* that *Meeruth walaon ka kata paani bhi nahi mangta hai.* Guys from western UP rock, and if they had been raised in Delhi, that's a lethal combination.

A weird-looking superhero in a golden and maroon outfit swirled on TV as Chotu watched, glued. The house phone rang and Chotu ignored it. Saturday forenoon was the best time for Chotu. His father, Joginder Mishra, was away from home, his mother was at her friends to discuss the latest issue of *Grihsobha*, and Bechu was at home, but busy with his CA exam preparations. The TV was in Chotu's control.

The landline phone rang again. Annoyed, Chotu picked it up.

"Bechu, your phone," said Chotu when he recognized Bhujang's trembling voice.

Bechu came running, and Chotu handed over the receiver. Bechu picked it. "What happened? Why are you calling at this time?" Bechu asked.

"*Bechu Bhaiya*, help me. This Sunil is crossing his boundary," Bhujang said.

"Who is Sunil?"

"That lean, smart guy." Bhujang hesitated after calling Sunil smart. "That lanky guy. You hit him for six once, and he glared at you."

"That new guy from Meerut? It's fine. Be easy with him. He is new, he does not know with whom he is messing around."

"*Bhaiya*, he is after Tunni. He also talks to other girls of the colony and passes vulgar comments," Bhujang exaggerated.

"Okay, take it easy. I have to focus on exams, but after four months, I can help you." Somehow Bechu felt uneasy. He never liked any stalkers. He used to think that he needed to protect his colony girls. A new guy, coming to this colony and passing vulgar remarks? He should be straightened.

Bechu looked at the TV. The weird superhero was preaching about avoiding tobacco products to kids.

✳

Tunni sauntered in her peacock green *salwar-kameez*. She had applied a red tiny dotted bindi which resembled the dawning sun of Sarsaiya ghat. At three o'clock in the afternoon, the streets of Kanpur were crowded with students. Students were preparing for medical and engineering entrance exams. She was with a group of girls, enjoying the attention of guys who were ogling at her.

Bhujang appeared at Bechu's gate. He pulled the latch of the iron gate and it made a metallic click. Hearing this, Bechu peeped from his first-floor balcony, and he gestured that he would be down in a minute.

Bechu opened the gate. He had two packages wrapped in newspaper. Bhujang looked at it and understood what it could be. Bechu handed one to Bhujang. Bhujang unwrapped the package. It was a *katta*, a locally made pistol. Bechu and Bhujang tucked them under their t-shirts.

"*Bhaiya*, I love her a lot. I cannot live without her," Bhujang admitted while walking on Kanpur Street.

Ignoring Bhujang's talk, Bechu took a turn to his left. Bhujang hesitated. Why did Bechu move towards the left? He should have gone straight for Ramdev Nagar for Paul's chemistry centre.

Paul sir was a renowned organic chemistry teacher. Rumours were that he had offers from Kota Bansal classes, but he had rejected these to serve in Kanpur.

"*Bhaiya*, why left? We need to go straight," Bhujang asked.

"We are going to Swaroop Nagar, Rishabh's apartment," Bechu said.

"Why are you calling that *angrez*? He cannot even slap a show-window dummy. Forget about berating someone," Bhujang declared.

Bechu looked at Bhujang. He again ignored him and moved forward.

"*Bechu Bhaiya*, we will be late," he added when Bechu stopped at Swaroop Nagar's apartment lobby. Bechu beckoned the security guard, who was in the dark-grey military shirt and a pair of yellowish dirty pyjamas. The guard immediately recognized Bechu and dialled a number through intercom.

After a while, Rishabh arrived. He noticed Bhujang, who was sulking in Rishabh's presence.

"Why don't you guys come up, have some tea?" Rishabh said.

"We are going to berate Sunil Chauhan," Bechu said

"That guy from Meerut, what did he do?" asked Rishabh.

"See, he knows him too. That day he was reciting poetry to him," Bhujang said to Bechu, glaring at Rishabh.

Bechu scowled at them and did not answer. He just walked ahead.

Puzzled, Bhujang and Rishabh followed him.

Rishabh noticed something was protruding from Bechu's waistline. He recognized that it was a gun, a desi *katta*. "Are you carrying a pistol?" Rishabh asked.

"He has already started crying," Bhujang objected. He showed his *katta* by pulling his t-shirt up a little.

"Elephants have different teeth for eating and for demonstrating," said Bechu. "Don't worry, we will not fire," he assured him.

"Don't even dare. I'm giving you a warning for your future," Rishabh said.

"If you want to sob, better you go back to Delhi. You will be a good fit there. This is Kanpur, and this is the city to show courage. The weak die like dogs here," Bhujang said to Rishabh and started walking ahead of them.

Bhujang increased his pace, as he had to reach Tunni's tuition on time.

✳

Paul sir was teaching about Kekule's benzene structure. He drew a six-carbon ring, a hexagon, and three double bonds. Tunni was busy in her own world. Ignoring the class, she doodled a heart. On one side she wrote 'Sunil' and on the other 'Khushbu', her real name. She separated their names with an arrow mark, which was penetrating the heart. She also imagined her full name, Khushbu Chauhan. It sounded very cool to her, far better than her dull name Kumari. She never liked her nickname as well. Khushi was a better nickname and she preferred that over Tunni, which was given by her parents.

Her bench-mate Pinky noticed her activities and teased her. When Tunni came out from her reverie, she saw that Sunil was standing outside of the class. He was in aviator sunglasses and trying to peep into the classroom to get a glimpse of Tunni. Tunni liked his style and his forwardness. The idea of meeting him at Ganga Ghat excited her. Would he try to kiss her? Thinking that, she got lost in her other dreams.

"Khushbu Kumari, can you tell me what is 1,3,5,7-Cyclooctatetraene?" Paul sir's stern voice echoed in the classroom.

Back to her senses, Tunni again glanced outside the window. Sunil was not there. She saw Bechu and Bhujang were looking for something. Tunni fumbled. She had forgotten everything about benzene and its stoichiometric relationships. She sensed why Bhujang was here.

"See, only a few students, hardly 5% can be admitted to IIT from this class, or even less. Clearly, I can see you don't want to be among them. Today, I noticed you are not paying attention. Like always, who does not pay attention, I send them out of my class."

Tunni startled. She stared at her own feet, the colour in her face deepening all the while. Her eyes welled up. Paul sir coughed a little, and Tunni walked out.

She heard a big noise. She noticed Bhujang was bellowing, "Catch that bastard…"

Sunil ran. He pushed aside aspirants to make some space. Bechu, Rishabh and Bhujang started chasing him. Bhujang struggled running in his Hawaiian *chappal*. He removed them and held them in his hand, and tossed them in the air. There was a safety pin attached to them, maintaining a grip. Bhujang threw them at Sunil, but Sunil ducked.

Sunil snatched an organic chemistry book, L.G. Wade, from a student and threw it at Rishabh. Rishabh ducked, but his head banged into the electricity pole. He lagged behind in the chase.

Sunil moved like a serpent. He sprinted and slithered through the zig-zagging Kanpur Street crowd while looking back at Bechu and Bhujang.

Bhujang picked a pebble up from the street and threw it at Sunil, but unfortunately, he hit a newspaper hawker on his routine paper distribution. The hawker pulled out his red *gamcha*, wiped his head and grabbed Bhujang by his collar. He spat out his pan, and his tinted teeth glittered. "*Sala*, trying to be a brawler? *Rangbaaz banta hai?*" the hawker said in a hoarse voice and slapped Bhujang.

"Bhujang, Run!" Bechu said and sprinted away. Bechu came running in between and pushed the hawker. He was not in a mood to fight a guy who was muscular and taller than them. Also, they needed to chase Sunil.

Meanwhile, out of breath, Sunil was having a rest and getting his energy back. He was holding his stomach tightly. He saw Bechu and Bhujang running again and trying to cross the street. Sunil looked at the alley and smiled. He was near the DAV college hostel. He sprinted.

Running desperately to save his life, Sunil banged the iron gate of the college hostel. Metal clanged, and Sunil fell to the ground. A whiff of dust swirled. He held his stomach, and a pain curled within.

Bechu and Bhujang came and started kicking him. Sunil bellowed with pain.

"*Madharchod,* will you stalk a girl from our colony?" Bhujang snarled. He did not realize he was in front of the boy's hostel gate.

Rishabh came running. He was panting. Somehow, he managed to pace them.

"Bechu *Bhai,* I made a mistake, leave me now," Sunil implored.

"From now onwards, Tunni is your sister," Bechu declared.

"And I'm your Jija," Bhujang kicked again. "Now say, '*Tunni Didi*,'" Bhujang leaned down and slapped Sunil.

"*Tunni Didi,*" Sunil bellowed and cried, clenching his stomach.

A few students saw this brawl at the gate and started gathering. They moved forward slowly, trying to ascertain if the guy at the gate was among their own.

Sunil saw that around twenty students were moving towards the gate now. This gave him courage. A few students ran to their rooms and returned with hockey sticks.

Rishabh noticed this. He whispered, "Bechu, let's go."

Sunil got some confidence. He sneered. His body language changed. He got up and dusted his jeans. He looked into Bechu's eyes. "Do you know, I'm the biggest *bahenchod* of this area," said Sunil. He slapped Bhujang and looked directly into Bechu's eyes.

Bechu tried to pull out his *katta.* He wanted to use it, but Rishabh came and grabbed his hand. He beckoned and gestured through his eyes to not make this mistake.

Sunil and his friends came very near to them. Rishabh shouted, "Bechu, run."

Within a second, the chase was reversed. Now Bechu, Rishabh, and Bhujang were running, and Sunil was chasing them with his twenty friends. This time, Rishabh was faster than all of them. They took an alley and disappeared.

Sunil and his hostel friends saw police patrolling the vehicle and Inspector Nikesh. Sunil's friends scurried away. No matter how big of a goon you are during your student life, you always want to stay away from the police.

Nikesh, an inspector of police, looked at the students but ignored them.

Bechu, Bhujang and Rishabh came back to their own colony. Rishabh saw that a big truck was parked across from Bechu's house, and workers were unloading furniture from it. Shatrughan Singh was giving directions.

Seeing the bustle, they walked ahead towards Gupta's shop, which was across from Tunni's house. It was mutual consent that first, they had to hide the *desi katta*.

Bhujang saw that Tunni was walking back from tuition. She looked disappointed. Her first date was a dud. She looked at Bhujang. A feeling of disgust ran through her stomach for him.

Slowly, all three, without speaking a word, moved ahead. Bechu pulled out his revolver from his waistline, which was tucked behind, to hold it safely. Bechu saw two girls come out of Gupta's shop. They were gleeful. The girl in bottle-green salwar-kameez with peacock blue border caught his attention. Happiness is contagious, especially when it's beaming through a beautiful girl. It brings an avalanche to a guy's life. Bechu's eyes met with hers, and the girl blushed. This was the first stone to fall in the avalanche. Bechu's world became slow. But the girl noticed the gun in his hand. She looked at Bechu again. Petrified, she moved her eyes away.

They took an alley next to Tunni's house to reach Azad Maidaan, where they played cricket. Rishabh and Bhujang were panting.

"Who was that girl?" Bechu asked first. He ignored the first trivial issue.

Rishabh ignored him. He wanted to talk about the main issue. "Why the hell did you pull out your gun?"

"I wanted to talk about the same thing. Why did you stop me?" Bechu fumed. "For the first time in my life, I had to run away like a coward." Bechu's face was red with anger. Within a second, he forgot about the girl and the moment that he had felt was love at first sight.

"What if the gun fired by mistake?" Rishabh said with concern, "You should not trust these weapons."

"How many times do I have to say that this was just to scare them? One shot in the air and they all might have shit in their pants!"

"You might have heard many tragic stories where people blew their own or others' brain out. You have not even received training to handle a gun. And this stupid one is not licensed. Have you heard about the Arms act? Did you see Inspector Nikesh while running back? He can put you behind bars just for possessing this."

Rishabh's logical argument irritated Bhujang more. "Just shut up!" he shouted at Rishabh. "I saw you, how you chickened out. Bloody coward!" Bhujang mocked.

"Bhujang, let it go," Bechu said.

"I don't understand why the hell you take the side of this shithead. You know him, right? He is a big sissy. To be a man, you need to act like a man. And this guy thinks that playing the guitar, talking in a stupid Delhi accent, and humming some English songs will make him one?" Bhujang snarled.

"Bhujang, you are crossing the line," Rishabh warned.

"Do you know Bechu? The day you know him, you will start hating him too."

Rishabh slapped Bhujang. Bhujang hit him back. They both jumped on each other. Rishabh always loathed a fight, but this time he did not want to spare Bhujang.

"Stop it, you pigs! Started fighting again," Bechu snarled. "Bhujang, apologize."

"Sorry," Bhujang said obediently. He never knew why he followed the command of Bechu. He always followed him; still, he could not count himself as Bechu's best friend.

"Rishabh, your turn!"

"For what?" Rishabh fumed. His lean and tall body was swaying with anger. "We both, Bechu and I, are running on Kanpur Street for your girlfriend. Sorry, *Chamiya*, that is the appropriate word you might be looking for." He continued, "We are fighting for your *maal*. That stupid girl does not have any idea that you like her, and never will."

"She is not stupid. She is preparing for JEE," Bhujang's eyes welled up.

"It does not matter. The crux is, I am wasting my time, Bhujang. I came with you guys because I consider you as my friend. Why should this fucking love triangle bother me? Between you, Tunni and whatever that guy's named – Sunil. I came because real manhood is not beating someone to a pulp. A real man stands with a friend. And I was fucking standing with you on this hot summer day."

Bhujang was looking at his feet. Tears made the soil wet.

"And the guy who is flunking his B.A. History exam even after taking history tuition, please don't lecture," Rishabh concluded. He glared at Bhujang and walked away.

Bhujang's throat choked up. He looked at Bechu and wanted to say something, but not a single word came out. The harsh words about failing exams were his weak point. His whole educational life and scene revolved in his mind. He remembered how he used to be a senior of Bechu, but once in the fifth grade, he had a year drop. The school principal gave his father the option to move ahead in the next class with grace marks, promising that he would focus on his studies. But his father requested the principal that Bhujang should repeat his year. He should be kept back in the same class.

Bhujang's life turned upside down. When he came back to school, all his friends had moved to the next class. They disowned the failed Bhujang. That year, he had entered the same grade five, which he loathed. Every eye was looking at him, failed boy. He lowered his eyes and walked past the first bench, which used to be his regular seat. His bench-mate was not there. He did not dare to look at that bench, and without looking at any, he sat down on the last bench. His confidence was shattered. There he found his junior and colony mate, Bechu. Bhujang started liking Bechu. He never asked how he failed. He welcomed him like a new student in the class. He never reminded him that he had read the same chapter or solved the same mathematics problems. But one thing had changed with Bhujang, the eyes which had seen the dream to become a fighter pilot now dreamt nothing. He just wanted to have immense power to crush the teeth of his schoolmates who used to tease him as a failure.

"See, you both are my friends. I don't understand why you loathe each other," Bechu's voice broke Bhujang's spurn. "Stop crying. It's the first time I'm seeing Schwarzenegger crying."

"What Negar?" Bhujang asaked.

"Ignore it, just think that it's Sunny Deol of Hollywood," Bechu smirked.

"You might be thinking of him as a friend, but I don't. You go home, you have to prepare for your exams."

✳

Bechu traipsed back home. He was aghast that his two friends had fought. It was also the first time he had ever had to run away like a coward. It was a bad day... He had promised himself that he would study a minimum of six to seven hours a day, but it was already six in the evening, and he had hardly finished a topic on indirect taxation – one of the CA final subjects that Bechu never liked.

When he reached the gate, he witnessed that Shatrughan Singh, the contractor, Bechu's new tenant, and his two henchmen were hassling with truck drivers and labourers. He remembered how his father had warned him about these henchmen, and Shatrughan had promised they would never be seen in this colony.

"Oh, it's the same guy, the gun rowdy," a sweet baby like voice got his attention. He saw the girl, who was there at Gupta's shop, in the bottle-green salwar-kameez.

"Oh Rimjhim, our father has rented a house in a rowdy's colony," Rakshita, Rimjhim's sister, said.

"It's all because of you. Your *fuddu aashiq*, Uma Pandey, came while he was drunk and screamed. Babuji fired his rifle, and the colony people asked him to leave."

"He is a loser. But now think, here rifles and guns are normal. Think, if same things happen, everything will be okay," Rakshita giggled. She saw Bechu open their gate and move towards the stairs. "Oh, he lives here!" Rakshita shrieked, astonished.

Bechu stared at them when he heard Rakshita's screeching voice. He saw Rimjhim was hiding behind her sister. He came forward.

"I'm your landlord," Bechu said and smiled. Bechu's heart pounded again. He controlled his emotions, but thousands of curious butterflies somersaulted in his stomach. "My name is Bechu – ahh, Amit Mishra," he corrected himself.

"I'm Rakshita, and she is Rimjhim. She is my elder sister but behaves like the younger one." Rakshita reached out her hand to Bechu to shake his.

Bechu knew that one of the girls among them was Rakshita. He had heard her name from the buffoon boy Uma Pandey when he had visited Bechu a week ago, as he remembered.

"Rimjhim, it's a nice and unique name. Sounds like the sound of the first fresh rain," Bechu made eye contact with Rimjhim.

"But Bechu is such a bad name!" Rakshita interrupted.

"Let it be, Bechu is very interesting and unique too," Rimjhim muttered and smiled at Bechu. She squinted her eyes and uniquely quivered her nose. Her nose ring glittered, which gave Bechu goosebumps.

Bechu looked for more words, but nothing occurred to him. He thought for a few seconds and felt that the best idea was to stride ahead into his house and avoid any stupid things he may say and ruin his impression in front of the most beautiful girl he had seen. He smiled and scurried backwards and vanished quickly.

"Oh Didi, this guy is so cute. Should I hit on him?" Rakshita teased Rimjhim.

"Shut up!" Rimjhim blushed.

The next day Bechu's alarm rang at 5:30 am, and he pushed the snooze button. He rubbed his eyes and recalled planning to study "Corporate Law and Secretarial Practice." The exam was in November, and he had four months.

He picked a question bank guide and glanced through past question papers. In the last exam, he had done reasonably well in this subject. It was good to start a morning with the known topics. He pulled out his green highlighter and underlined the requirements of Section 269 with Schedule XIII to the Companies Act, 1956. He read it and yawned. Bechu looked at his watch – it was six-fifteen. He thought he could sleep for a few minutes.

Sumati, Bechu's mother, came into the room after completing her puja. It was eight-thirty now, and she was worried that Bechu's father would finish the newspaper by nine and ask for Bechu. She switched off the fan.

She went ahead to the corner table to switch off the computer monitor, which was still flickering. She looked at the wallpaper. It was a family photo. Joginder Mishra, her husband, was happy and smiling. She was in a blue dotted saree with her three children, Bechu, Chotu and Shruti. Her eyes welled up, and she was filled with emotions. She switched off the monitor. A few tears rolled down her face, and she wiped them off.

"It's nine in the morning, and this nawab sahib is still sleeping. I'm not sure what he will do with his future," Joginder screamed, standing at the door.

"He was studying the whole night," Sumati defended Bechu with a typical motherly response.

"I don't know what kind of exam or course he is attempting; he never succeeds," Joginder frowned. "Never try to defend him. I heard the stuttering trill of the router last night. He must have connected to the internet."

Bechu got up again when he heard a doorbell ring. He quickly checked the clock on his table. It was nine-thirty. He adjusted his superman shorts and pushed his books aside. He looked at the teacup on the table. He touched it, and it was cold. He heard his mother open the door.

"I brought *kheer*. It was the first day in the house, so Mother made some and she asked me to give it to you," Bechu heard a sweet voice say. It was Rimjhim.

Bechu wanted to go to the kitchen and get a glimpse of Rimjhim. Drinking a glass of water was a better idea.

"Have you set all your furniture?" Sumati asked.

Bechu entered the kitchen and opened the fridge. He wrenched the bottled cap and gave a side look to Rimjhim. He saw his mother frown, and Rimjhim giggled. He looked down: he was still in tiny Superman shorts, which were more like underwear.

"I'm going now, Aunty," Rimjhim said while holding back her laughter. She blushed.

Bechu realized that he was the object of her laughter. He ran away. After a few minutes, Bechu returned, wearing jeans.

"Is breakfast ready?" he asked his mother. He did not find Rimjhim and was disappointed.

"Breakfast! It's time for lunch," his mother muttered.

"You give entry to anyone in the house. You should think about something. You have two young adult sons," Bechu said to cover up his embarrassment.

"Two! I have only one adult son who wanders around in underwear. Chotu is still a kid!" Sumati grinned.

"Don't underestimate your youngest lad. The caterpillar is ready to become a butterfly."

"Okay, that girl was our new tenant's daughter. She is not anyone."

"Oh, thanks for letting me know." Bechu avoided mentioning that he had been introduced to her the evening before. If you like someone, better stay away from any topic related to that person. This is how the human brain works. It wants to deny the fact.

"Help them. We live like a family. She is a year older than you. She is like your elder sister," Sumati said.

Bechu hated this comment. Why do Indian mothers want to make all good-looking females into their son's sisters? And what was the problem if a girl was a year older than him? She was not his sister. She was beautiful.

"What are you thinking?" Sumati asked.

"No, nothing. I had only one sister, and no one can take her place. This girl is only my tenant, not my sister," Bechu declared. He found solid reasoning to shut everyone up. He did not want sister business with Rimjhim. He hated to play this card, but it was better to stop his mother from calling Rimjhim his sister.

✳

Bechu locked himself in for the next few days to complete his syllabus. He did not hear back from Rishabh and Bhujang. He missed Rishabh a lot. He wanted to know how his preparation was going, what his opinion was on group A, management accounting. He revised his concepts on inventories control, receivables, and credit policy thrice and solved a few problems. After three to four days of continuously following his study schedules, his brain was ready to explode. To get some peace of mind, he thought of Chotu.

Bechu came out of his room and asked his mother where Chotu was. She directed him towards a room.

"That room was locked," asked Bechu.

"Yes, but Chotu cleaned it and made it as his study room. He said you disturb him," said Mother.

Bechu hesitated first but entered the room without knocking on the door or making any noise.

Chotu was studying with concentration. He was engrossed in his books. Bechu snatched the book.

"Give my book back to me!" Chotu screamed.

"Let me know what you are reading with so much concentration. Is it a comic book?" Bechu asked.

"Just give it back and don't dare to intrude my privacy," Chotu snarled.

"Privacy my foot," Bechu smirked and examined his book. He saw, in the middle of the book, there was a semi-nude picture of Pamela Anderson. Bechu gasped and whistled. "What is that?" Bechu said. "This is for adults, and you are still a kid." Bechu waved the picture in the air and threatened, "Mother should see what her topper son is doing!"

"Bechu, please, don't tell this to Papa or Ma," Chotu wept.

"Okay, then you have to go to Rishabh's house and tell him that I want to meet him."

"Why? Did you guys fight again?" asked Chotu.

"No, I was just busy with my studies. Will you help me?"

"Okay, I will," said Chotu. He still did not believe that Bechu had assigned him such an easy task.

"Where is your piggy bank?" Bechu demanded.

Chotu gestured at his table. Now he had realized that talking with Rishabh was just the first requirement. He had to make more enormous sacrifices for Pamela.

Bechu picked the piggy bank up and smashed it, and coins and notes dashed on the floor. He took all the money without even counting. "It's mine. Take these ten rupees note and go bring some *patang* and *manja*," Bechu ordered.

It was five in the evening. The sun was still shining on the western horizon, and the sky had turned pinkish. The late afternoon July monsoon downpour had made the air cooler. Chotu had bought some kites and *manja*. He was busy rolling into a *lataai*.

"Can you teach me how to give *kanni*?" Chotu asked.

"Not yet, you may cut your fingers. These threads are so sharp," Bechu said as he pulled the string, and the purple kite took a sharp dive. It overlapped a blue kite. Bechu unleashed the thread reel. The kites' threads met, and their threads whooshed. The blue kite quivered in the sky. It got free.

"*Wo kata*," Chotu screamed and smiled. His bunny teeth on display.

Bechu rolled back the reel, and his kite soared upwards in the sky. He looked right and saw that a bottle-green salwar-kameez with other dresses were hung on a wire.

"That's Rimjhim *didi's*. She put her clothes on the clothesline a few hours ago to get dry," Chotu informed, anticipating his elder brother's curiosity.

"You are not going to call her *didi*," Bechu smirked.

"Why? She is older than me. I should call her *didi*."

"If you start calling every girl *didi,* who are you going to marry?"

"Why should I marry?" asked Chotu

"We all have to marry. You have to marry when you become an adult."

"Why I cannot marry someone now?"

"Because you ask so many questions. You can marry when you have all the answers and no questions," said Bechu.

Chotu pondered on it. His brother had a point. Meanwhile, they heard two girls striding up the stairs, giggling at each other. Bechu's heart took a giant leap. Now his heart quivered like a free kite in the sky.

Rimjhim and her sister appeared at the terrace through the staircase door. Rimjhim was in white salwar and white kameez with a red dot bindi. Rakshita was in shorts and a t-shirt.

Chotu gawked. He had never seen a young girl in shorts.

"This Rakshita is very beautiful. When I become an adult, I will marry her, *bus jawan hone ki der hai*," Chotu whispered to Bechu.

Bechu smiled. "*Pahle yeh patang sambhaal tab apni jawani sambahliyo*," he muttered, and handed the thread reel to Chotu. Chotu took the thread reel, the *lataai*, reluctantly. Bechu smiled at Rimjhim and strolled towards her.

"Why, Mr Bechu, enjoying the wind after a fresh rain?" Rakshita beckoned Rimjhim and grinned.

Rimjhim laughed.

"You smile a lot," Bechu said.

"What to do? We were all watching *Superman* on Cartoon Network. It's a funny series, you know," Rakshita taunted. She put her left hand on her mouth and cackled.

"Rakhsita, shhh," hissed Rimjhim.

Rimjhim must have talked about their embarrassing moment to Rakshita. Bechu's confidence shattered, and his heart sank. *Why do girls tell each and every thing to their best friends or sisters?* Bechu thought to himself. He collected his crumbled courage. "I like The Power-puff Girls," Bechu smiled.

"Which one, the eldest one, Blossom, or younger one, Bubbles?" Rakshita again interrupted and pointed at her when she mentioned Bubbles.

"I like maturity, so of course, the elder one," Bechu looked into Rakshita's eyes, teasing her, and then gazed at Rimjhim. Rakshita and Rimjhim both blushed.

"By the way, the kheer was delicious. Did you cook it?" Bechu took a step forward.

"Rimjhim, let's go," Rakshita pulled Rimjhim. "*Superman* is starting soon on Cartoon Network." They trudged on the wet staircase.

Bechu was stunned. He wanted to talk to Rimjhim, to know what she liked or disliked. To win and dwell in a girl's heart, you need to win the heart of her friend or sister. Here, Rakshita had started teasing him and making fun of him. It was a good sign, he thought. He smiled on his knowledge of the art of seduction. A book he had read at Rishabh's house. Any knowledge is knowledge. It never goes in vain.

"I'm also going to watch the cartoon," Chotu stomped off and handed the reel to Bechu.

✸

Rimjhim lit a *diya* and prayed for a minute. She mixed *roli* and *chandan* and applied them to her forehead and neck. She turned toward Rakshita, who was reading the Hindi version of *Stardust* magazine.

"Why did we run away? I wanted to talk with him."

"Hold on, miss, wait for the right time. I have been with many guys and made them run after me. Clearly, he likes you, so let the fruit ripen and the curiosity rise," Rakshita raised her brow.

"He seems to be a nice guy."

"All guys are nice," Rakshita turned the page. She glanced through the gossip column called *Nita ki chatar-patar.*

"For a moment, I felt like he should make a move and hold my hand," Rimjhim looked at her wrist. The red bangle clanked. She touched her wrist.

"The guy who was making a move and holding your hand twice, you are not even giving him any value," Rakshita smiled.

"You better focus on your movie gossip, not on my personal life." Rimjhim threw a pillow at her. She knew Rakshita was talking about Guddu Shukla but was probably not aware that Rimjhim never liked him.

✸

An alarm clock rang. Instead of pushing the snooze button, this time, Bechu woke up right away. The morning sunshine filtered through his window. He picked up the corporate law book and revised a few cases. Banking

Regulation Act 1949. He yawned. The dull topic made him sleepy again.

Bechu's mother came and placed a cup of tea on the table with bread and jam. Bechu picked it up, and he got the familiar aroma of the breakfast he used to carry for his school tiffin. It reminded him of Chotu.

"Is Chotu getting ready for school?" Bechu asked.

"Yes, he is. I prepared his tiffin, so I shared some with you."

Bechu went to Chotu's room. Chotu, in navy blue shorts and a white shirt, was combing his hair. Bechu beckoned him. Chotu nodded begrudgingly.

Chotu entered the large apartment complex. He looked for a guard who was not available. Chotu waited for a few minutes. He looked at his watch, a yellow digital one where the black numbers were blinking. It was a quarter to seven. Chotu was getting late.

Chotu opened the channelled gate lift and shut the door. He had to go to the third floor, but he pressed five. He smiled. The elevator reached the fifth floor. An aged man walked in. Chotu looked at him. The old man pushed floor zero, Chotu pressed three.

The old man looked at Chotu and frowned.

"Wanted to go to three but pressed five by mistake," Chotu said.

Chotu reached apartment 303. He read the door board, Late Vimlesh Khanna. He read twice and jumped to get the doorbell. It rang with a familiar Gayatri-mantra sound.

Rishabh opened the door in grey shorts and a dark blue round-neck t-shirt. He beckoned Chotu to follow him into his room. He saw the Macintosh green semi-transparent monitor.

"Is this an Apple computer?" Chotu asked.

"Yes."

"And you must have an internet connection as well," Chotu looked through the phone wire, which was connected through a CPU.

"Yes," Rishabh said.

"Can I open a website?"

"Which one?" Rishabh raised his brow.

"I have heard a lot about Savita Bhabhi," Chotu said without any expression. He sat on the chair next to the computer desk.

"Aren't you getting late for school?

"No, I left thirty minutes early, so that I could meet you. Bechu asked you to come and see him."

Rishabh nodded. He sighed. "Okay, I will come tomorrow evening."

"No, please open the website," Chotu pleaded.

"It's not for you," Rishabh smirked.

"Why everything is for adults? God knows when I will become an adult," Chotu groaned.

"Go to your school," Rishabh opened the door. He laughed loudly.

✳

The next evening, the fall breeze was a little dry. Rimjhim's mother was drying red chillies on the terrace. Rimjhim and Rakshita spread the chillies on a bedsheet.

"Next time, just buy pickles from the market. Why so much drama?" Rakshita advised her mother.

Rimjhim heard a metal clacking sound. She thought that it was Bechu, and she ran towards the railing. Rakshita followed.

"Ohh, we have not seen the superman for a week," Rakshita teased.

They saw a young man in jeans and a v-neck t-shirt open the gate. He was fair and average height, five foot seven. He looked up at the girls, ignored them and rocketed towards the stairs for Bechu's house.

"Oh boy, *gajab,* look at his attitude," Rakshita murmured. She blushed.

"Shh, shut up. You just need to see a handsome guy, and you start," Rimjhim said.

"So you do agree that he is hot?" Rakshita said.

"I would say average looking, but his attitude makes him attractive," Rimjhim remarked. "Anyway, how is your *ashiq-chaman-bahar* Umanath Pandey?" Rimjhim inquired further.

"Don't ask about him *Di*. He has been following me for the past two years. Whenever I come in front of him, his throat chokes. He cannot speak a word. I'm thinking, now I have to take a bold step."

"Why? Are you mad?" Rimjhim said.

"What can I do? I don't have many *ashiqs*. Whatever I have, I have to accept my fate and try my luck," Rakshita grinned.

She leaned over to get a better look, but the good-looking guy, Rishabh, knocked on Bechu's door and disappeared.

✳

Bechu's mother opened the door, and Rishabh touched her feet. She was delighted to see Rishabh after a long time.

Well-mannered Rishabh was her favourite among Bechu's friends.

"You have stopped coming to the house," she said.

"No, Auntie, I was just a little busy," Rishabh avoided eye contact.

"So busy that I'm seeing you after almost two years!" Sumati said and smiled. "I will make your favourite Shikanji. Bechu is there in his room."

✳

"Come sit here," Bechu gestured Rishabh to a stool when he entered the room. "Are you still upset?" asked Bechu, and he turned some pages of the book of cost management, a chapter on learning curve theory.

"This question came in the May exam. I don't think they will repeat it, so ignore it," Rishabh said.

"Don't change the topic. Are you still upset?"

Rishabh looked at the photo frame, the familiar Mishra family. Bechu, Chotu, Shruti, Uncle and Aunty. He felt that Shruti made eye contact with him.

"Why should I feel bad?" Rishabh said. His voice choked.

"*Bura maan ke kya ukhad lega?*" Bechu chuckled.

"You won't change," Rishabh said.

That was Bechu, always making him smile with his eerie humour.

Rishabh opened his bag zip and drew out some notes. He handed them to Bechu.

"What are these?" Bechu said.

"Notes on central excise law, custom valuation rules and custom acts,"

"No, I don't need it; I'm only appearing in one group this time. I chose Group 2."

"Why?"

"Want to focus on one group and improve my chances of passing," Bechu said.

"No, then it will take one more year for you to pass. It's a risk. I don't think Joginder Uncle can wait. He is impatient. Just focus on Advanced Accountancy, and you can pass. Last year your preparation was solid, and you missed by just a few marks."

"I'm unable to focus on multiple subjects. I'm dealing with my own problems," Bechu sighed.

"We all are dealing with some problems, Bechu. Problems will keep arising, so don't let them become an excuse. Just ignore this Bhujang."

"It's not about Bhujang."

"Then?"

"This guy Uma Pandey, he is circling our house on his stupid Rx100, for Rakshita."

"Oh, for your new tenants. I remember that joker. And your tenants are not innocent either. I saw them while coming in," Rishabh said. He raised his brow.

"No, they are nice girls," Bechu said with conviction.

Rishabh wanted to say something. But he held his thought for a minute. He then uttered his next few words carefully. "I have heard that Guddu Shukla is the guy who is after one of these girls."

"Who is Guddu Shukla?"

"Look, you don't need to be a protector for your tenants. Their parents are there for that job. You don't have to be the alpha male here. The final exam is in November. We have only ninety days. I'm planning to take only group one. You should try for both groups."

Bechu's nerves wracked. He ignored the advice. Guddu Shukla's name got under his skin. He had heard about Guddu Shukla before. As he reckoned, it was from Uma Nath Pandey.

DAV boys' hostel at Civil Lines was deserted at night. It was Saturday, and many residents were out to enjoy the weekend. The hostel bathroom was cold and whistling in the silence. Standing tall in front of the mirror, Guddu brushed his teeth and looked at the local desi graffiti on the bathroom wall, a few obscene doodles drawn in charcoal emphasizing human genitalia.

"Assholes!" Guddu smirked.

He peed and washed his hand. He tried to close the tap and wrenched it multiple times, but water droplets still leaked out. *"Bhenchod,"* he shook the tap vigorously,

Guddu removed his tucked '*janev*' and walked down the corridor. After a few steps, he heard a murmuring sound. It was from the same floor, further down in the passage. He sped up and stopped at room 13.

He stopped at the door, which was half ajar. He saw around five second-year M.A. students, senior to Guddu, interrogating a junior guy. The guy was lean and yellow in colour due to some unknown fear.

"What should we do with you?" A guy in his mid-thirties, Vinod Yadav, rubbed tobacco in his palm. "Why did you come to this college?"

"I came here for my studies," the junior replied. He lowered his gaze, and his shoulders drooped.

"Which subject?" Vinod Yadav asked further, sharing his *khaini* with others. "*Pahile naam batao bey.* Full good name?"

"Animesh Srivastava, people call me Lala. Came here to study Hindi Literature. I'm a B.A. first-year student," Lala said.

"So, *Lala Ji, koi Hindi Kavita sunaiye.* It has been a long time, I have heard any. Recite something like Kumar Vishwas," Vinod Yadav said.

Lala hesitated for a few seconds. Then he scanned the room. Around five seniors were looking at him lecherously. Lala closed his eyes. He recalled his favourite poem, which he had studied in tenth grade. It was about the spring season of braves. He had to be brave.

"*Aa rahi himalay se pukaar, hai uaddhi garajta baar-baar, praachi packshim bhu nav paar, sab puch rahe dig digant, veeron ka kaisa ho vasant...*"

"*Bhaag gaandoo*, stop this. Who wrote this?"

"Subharda Kumari Chauhan," Lala said.

"Who is that?" Vinod Yadav adjusted his seat. He was sitting on a desi pistol. He removed it from his pants and put it on the bed. The originally white bedsheet was brown. There must be some bed bugs, Lala thought. Vinod looked like a massive bug to him. For a moment, Lala wanted Vinod Yadav to become a bug, similar to Kafka's novel, *Metamorphosis*.

"She is a poet," Lala said. He swallowed his spit.

"*Bhaag betichod!* You don't even know how to rag properly. Is this a high school? It's a great Kanpur DAV college, and it's a hostel. His ragging should be epic," a guy in designer jeans and a see-through shirt said. His name was Rajiv Mahto.

For a moment, to Lala, Rajiv Mahto looked like a *gandoo*, a gay. The guy's dark brown nipples and bushy hair were protruding out from his shirt. Lala scanned him: the guy's zip was open, and his lips were red due to chewing excessive *gutkha*.

"Have you kissed anyone?" the guy in the transparent shirt asked.

Now the word epic was ringing in Lala's ear. Did he want to kiss him? Lala wiped his sweat. His lips quivered and became pale. "No."

"Sex?"

"No," Lala shuddered.

"Why, *jawani ufaan nahi marta kya?*" Rajiv Mahto asked in a thick Kanpuri accent.

All five guys in the room laughed.

"Why Mahto? *Iska gaand marogey ka?*" Vinod asked. He winked at Mahto.

Guddu was at the door and till now listening to this with patience. In the last university election, Vinod Yadav had tried his luck against Guddu but failed. Vinod was his arch-rival in university politics.

Guddu opened the room door and entered. He tore a packet of pan-masala and peppered it into his mouth, then flicked it away. "What the hell's going on here?" Guddu snarled like a lion.

There was silence for a moment. Guddu stared at the see-through shirt guy. Rajiv Mahto closed his top shirt button. The other guys stood from their chairs and wiped their sweaty hands on their trousers. One guy, though he was a senior, bowed slightly to Guddu in respect.

"Guddu, you better go. It's not related to you," Vinod Yadav said.

Guddu looked at Lala. Lala was scared. He felt as if God had come to rescue him. He felt how Draupadi might have felt when she saw Krishna when Dushasana was doing *cheerharana.*

"Then what kind of matter is mine?"

"Don't talk to your senior like this," Vinod Yadav gathered his remaining courage and spoke with attitude.

"*Jyada bhachar-bhachar kiye tho yahi senior-junior ek kar dengey.* Don't mess with me, Vinod. Just shut up and mind your business. You came here for your studies, and it's better you do that."

Vinod Yadav looked at the ceiling. The decades-old Khaitan fan was spinning slowly. He counted the blades, then sighed. He knew that he could not mess with Guddu Shukla. He looked at the floor and then spoke to Lala, "Get lost."

Lala came out of the room. He was not sure whether he should wait for Guddu, and thank him, or just leave. He decided to wait.

"*Aage se dhyaan rahe,*" Guddu warned Vinod and then he came back to the hostel corridor. Guddu noticed that Lala was waiting beside the next door.

"Go to room 21, and you will find a stove. Prepare some tea. You do know how to prepare tea, right?" Guddu Shukla ordered.

"Yes," Lala said reluctantly. He was surprised.

"Do you know how to remove *haldi* stains from a white shirt?" Guddu asked.

Lala nodded. Lala was not sure. He had escaped from one trouble and gotten caught in another; he was out of the frying pan, and now he was in the fire. Lala was sure that his next task was to wash Guddu's clothes. He was now Guddu's servant.

✳

In the courtyard of DAV college hostel, Uma Nath Pandey was busily narrating a film story. He was not a resident of this hostel, but he used to spend his time here.

"Have you seen *Tezaab*? It was hit only because of Chunky Pandey," Uma said enthusiastically. He was a great fan of Chunky Pandey because both shared the same surname, but secretly he used to like Ajay Devgan.

"Don't talk crap? It was a hit because of Madhuri, the '*ek-do-teen*' song," a hostel boy said. He was in a towel and a *sandow ganji*, and it looked like he came from the toilet a minute ago.

"*Beta*, when this movie released, you were in diapers. So just listen, and don't interrupt."

Lala was washing clothes on the ground floor. He had soaked clothes in a plastic bucket. He was listening to the conversation with keen interest.

"*Uma Bhaiya* is right, that '*so gaya yeh jahan*' song is epic," Lala interrupted. He circled his right hand, depicting that he was driving a car.

"See one more Chunky Pandey fan, *kasam se Lala*. If you were a girl, I would have married you right now, right here." Uma winked at him.

"And Nilam and Chunki's *jodi* was the best. That *Ghar Ka Chiraag* movie song, *tutak-tutak-tutak tutiya*," Lala added. His chest was thumping with pride. He had scored some points in Uma's heart.

"And Chunky Pandey is a *chutiya*," a hostel resident added.

All laughed, and Lala followed. Uma Pandey frowned and stared at Lala.

"Have you washed all the clothes, or should I ask *Guddu Bhaiya* to add more?" Uma blurted.

They all heard the sound of a Bajaj Pulsar bike. Sunil Chauhan got down from it, putting his sunglasses in his pocket, and the bike key swirling around his index finger like Krishna holding his Sudarshan Chakra. He was furious, and there was a black bruise on his left eye.

"Where is *Guddu Bhaiya*?" Sunil asked Uma and the other hostel residents.

❋

In room number 21, Guddu was sitting on a four-poster. He picked a Time classes CAT prep book and tried to solve some quants questions. He read the question twice and then checked the wall clock.

"Lala," Guddu shouted, "put rice on the stove. It is eleven now."

Lala stopped washing clothes and ran towards Guddu's room. Sunil heard the voice, and he followed Lala. Uma took the lead and ushered them. They all stopped at the door of room number 21. Uma and Sunil looked at each other. They hesitated for a bit. Uma showed some courage. He knocked on the door and entered the room.

"Sorry to interrupt *Guddu Bhaiya*, Sunil has come," Uma said.

Guddu scanned Sunil and Uma. He noticed Sunil's bruises and cut marks on his right eye.

"Bechu Mishra and Bhujang had beaten him black and blue. Sunil was in the hospital for a week," Uma added.

"So, what can I do? Should I worship you? I have heard that he got beaten to a pulp at our hostel gate, then Vinod Yadav's gang chased them off. I also know it's because of a girl, Tunni," Guddu said. He did not look at Sunil while speaking and pencilled an answer on a mock-test paper.

Lala entered the room. He was scared, as he was late.

"Lala, prepare three cups of tea," Guddu ordered.

There was silence for a few minutes while Guddu solved the quants problems. Sunil looked at Uma for further help. Uma put his finger on his lips and indicated to Sunil to keep quiet for a few more minutes.

"I've flunked this MBA entrance exam the past two years. This year I have to crack it," Guddu looked at Uma. "How is your IIT-JEE preparation?"

"Going on, *Bhaiya*," Uma said.

"I heard you were discussing the movie *Tezaab*. One day I will pour a bottle of *tezaab* on your head."

Uma was silent again. Lala bought teacups and gave a cup to Guddu. Then he handed a cup each to Sunil and Uma. He filtered the tea leaves and kept the fourth cup for himself. Guddu noticed it.

"Sale, *mere baap ke baraat main aaye ho*? Who asked you to drink tea? Keep that cup on the table and go prepare rice," Guddu ordered.

Lala fumbled and started washing rice in a bowl.

"*Bhaiya*, I love Tunni. This Bhujang loves her too, so got help from Bechu in vengeance," Sunil bleated.

"*Gaand main guda nahi hai prem karne ka to kaahe ungli karte ho*? Now you should get your ass kicked," Guddu said.

"Now translate it into English," Guddu said.

"Which one?" Sunil asked.

"That *guda* dialogue," Guddu barked.

Sunil hesitated for a while. He looked to Uma again for help.

"If you don't have muscle in your ass, then why are you fingering ..." Sunil stammered.

"Your own asshole," Uma completed the sentence for him.

"Very good. Now listen. You jumped in this shithole. I have done enough of this university politics, *lafuabaazi*, this *maar-peet* and *gundagardi*. Now it's time to think about my future. I have decided to crack the MBA exam, get a decent job, and marry Rimjhim. So, spare me. I need to focus and concentrate. Next floor, you will find Vinod Yadav, ask him. He will help you guys and can save your ass from Bhujang and Bechu Mishra," Guddu said.

Guddu picked up the book again and started reading the next set of questions. He circled the pencil in his fingers and gestured for Sunil and Uma to go away.

"*Guddu Bhaiya*, you should be aware that Rimjhim and her family moved to a different house," Uma said. He hesitated while sharing the news.

"What? When and Why?" Guddu was now curious. He closed his book.

Guddu got up from his four-poster and sat on the chair. He put the book on the table and crossed his leg. He looked at Uma and Sunil, then raised his brow.

"*Bhaiya*, that day when we – I mean I screamed Rakshita's name in front of her house. You must have remembered, Shatrughan Singh, Rimjhim's father, fired a rifle. After that, the colony people were unhappy, and the landlord asked them to move to a different location."

Guddu put the pencil in his mouth. He tore open a packet of *gutkha* and sprinkled it on his palm. Slowly he dusted it off and put it in his mouth.

"Where are the Singh family now?" Guddu asked.

Uma looked at Sunil. His heart pounded.

"*Ji, Bhaiya*, at Bechu Mishra's house," said Sunil.

"What! the same Bechu Mishra who beat you?" Guddu looked at Sunil.

Sunil nodded. "*Bhaiya*, it's fine. I will ask Vinod Yadav," Sunil jeered.

"*Aye*, Mr Meerut. *Gaand ziyada moti naa karo*. The husky voice you are using to woo girls, I will shove that baritone voice up your asshole. This is my case now." Guddu stared at him with his big eyes. "Uma, get all details about him. I want to know when Bechu eats, what time he responds to the call of nature, everything. I don't want a love triangle in my story. We have to end it now."

Sunil and Uma got up to leave. They bowed their head to Guddu in respect.

"Meerut, wait. Do one thing. Go out more with Tunni." Guddu handed a five-hundred-rupee note to Sunil. "Go watch movies with her. Go on dates and make this guy Bhujang jealous."

Sunil smiled. "She prefers the name Khushi," he whispered as if sharing a secret.

"I don't care what she calls herself" then he turned towards Uma, "and Uma Pandey, you have been running after my *saali*, sister-in-law, for the past two years. Show some *gudaa*, courage. It's time to escalate your love story."

Guddu ordered his disciples. This was what he had learnt during his tenure in student politics. A leader always gets the work done smartly. He never makes his own hands dirty.

The next day, Uma bought *ladoos* from a shop near Devki Cinema. He was full of energy. *Guddu Bhaiya* was right. You never know; Rakshita might be looking for an escalation. He was still thinking that he would propose to Rakshita once he passed IIT-JEE. Like Guddu had plans to propose Rimjhim after completing his MBA.

Uma Pandey had tried the JEE exam thrice. Once, he got admission into Carpet Technology. But due to low rank, he had skipped the admission. He wanted to study computer science. Anyway, today, he was in a decisive and determined mood. He had to start pursuing Rakshita. Instead of being a passive lover, he had to be an active one.

"What will you do with these *Thaguu ke ladoos*?" Sunil asked.

"I will give them to Rakshita," Uma said.

"How? Have you talked to her? Let her know that you like her?" Sunil asked.

"No, but she knows," Uma muttered.

Sunil never understood how in Kanpur this was possible. A guy liked a girl but never expressed his feelings to her; still, the girl knew. He was unaware of this small-town telepathy. Did all girls in India have these unsaid rules and awareness, or was it the speciality of Kanpur? He did not know. For Sunil, wooing a girl was always easy. The more he gargled with *fitkari*, potash alum, the more girls were attracted to his voice. Then he had added the regular grooming regimen that had worked like icing on the cake.

"Okay, I will go to that colony and see Tunni, come with me. You can sit at the magazine shop and wait for Rakshita. Try your luck. You may have to repeat it many times. Eventually, you will find the correct time to impress her. Seducing a girl is a test cricket match, you must wait for a loose ball. If she comes to the shop, then give her your stupid gift and strike a conversation with confidence," Sunil suggested.

Uma felt jealous of Sunil's confidence, and he did not like that Sunil called his gift 'stupid'. He had seen Shatrughan Singh buying *ladoos* from this shop with Rakshita many times. He had seen Rakhista's gleaming eyes, and he knew

Rakshita loved *ladoos*. Now, Sunil had a girl, and he was acting smart.

He remembered when they had met Sunil first and had a few drinks with him. Uma had introduced Sunil to *Guddu Bhaiya*, and it was Uma who had suggested Tunni to Sunil.

"I understood, now don't fly high. Let's go to Barra," Uma said. He jumped onto the back seat, holding the *ladoo* packet in one hand and the bike's backseat handle in another.

"We just need to be conscious of Bhujang," Sunil said.

"What about Bechu Mishra?"

"Don't worry, he is not a threat until…."

"Until what?"

"Until *Guddu Bhaiya* instigates trouble. There is an adage in Hindi, putting a hand in a beehive."

"*Guddu Bhaiya* does not invite trouble. He is trouble. And about Bechu, leave *Bhaiya, ussey humara jhaant bhi nahi darta*," Uma said, like a *bhakt*.

"Fine. I don't care. We will park the bike in front of Shyam Nagar, then walk up to the street. We will go separately, and when our work is done, meet me near the cricket field. I don't want those people noticing us," Sunil explained the plan.

The next few days, Uma frequently droned around Rakshita's house on his Yamaha RX100 bike. He had courage because he had unconditional love from Guddu Shukla. After a few tries, he saw Rakshita one day. She was in a lavender-pink kameez and white *churidar*. Her matching white *dupatta* fluttered, so Uma's heart revved faster than his RX100 bike engine.

Holding a vegetable bag in her hand, she took a long stride. Uma saw *shalgam*, turnip, in the bag; he never liked it, but it resembled his heart. Uma rummaged in his backpack for the *ladoos*. He took the box out and opened it. The *ladoos* were stale.

Uma looked around. There was no trace of Bhujang or Bechu. The area was safe and secure for him. Rakshita saw him, and her heart pounded.

Though Rakshita was not scared of Uma, today, Uma looked determined, and she thought to test the waters. Rakshita stood in front of Uma when he was putting his bike on the stand.

"What's the matter?" Rakshita asked.

"Nothing… nothing," Uma stammered. He wiped his head with his forearm.

"You have been stalking me for two years. What's your next move?"

Escalate your love story. Uma remembered *Guddu Bhaiya's* message. Here, Rakshita was escalating it.

"*Aage kya karein!*" said Uma. He had no clue. He involuntarily looked at Rakshita's bosom.

"Don't think lewd. I'm not asking for something else or to do anything."

"No, No. I'm just..." Uma was lost in his words. In nervousness, he was not even able to complete his sentences.

"That night, it was you who screamed my name. Right?" Rakshita asked.

"Yes." Uma looked down at the road coyly.

"Are you sure? That was a brave act. You don't look like one who can pull that off."

After hearing this, Uma got some confidence back. He stood tall and spread his chest. He brushed his sloppy look.

"I think we should talk more and get to know each other," Rakshita said.

"Do you have a phone number?"

"Landline, yes, but Papa or Ma picks it up most of the time. You should buy a mobile. I can call you on it."

"Mobile phone is expensive. But I will arrange for it," Uma assured her. His smile was now wider.

Rakshita noticed a Chunky Pandey's sticker on Uma's bike. She giggled. "Are you a Chunky Pandey fan?"

"Yes."

"But now he does not do any movies. Are you okay with Ajay Devgan's movies?" Rakshita said.

"I'm fine with any movies."

"I don't watch any movies, but I love Ajay Devgan" Rakshita continued. "Let's watch *Qayamat*. Have you heard that song, '*Yeh Ladka Bahot Yaad Aata Hai*'? That is from this movie. We can go tomorrow, Thursday. Afternoon, the theatre will not be crowded. Book tickets in advance. *Gunjan main lagi hai*." Rakshita was excited.

"Okay," Uma nodded.

"Wait, it has some kissing scenes I have seen in trailers. It comes on Zee TV *Dekh ke tharak mat jana*. You look a little naughty."

Uma was astonished. For the past few days, he had thought about how he would give these *ladoos* to Rakshita. What he would tell her. And here he was. He had landed his first date in Gunjan Cinema.

"Now, don't grin and shut your gob. Bechu Mishra can come any time. *Futto yahan se*," Rakshita ordered.

"*Darte nahi hain hum Bechu se*. I'm not afraid at all." Uma looked into Rakshita's eyes. He revved his bike.

✳

The following day, the weather was gloomy. The monsoon was at an end. Uma Nath Pandey had visited the barbershop twice. First, he had gone to a high-end salon and paid 250 rupees for a shave and haircut. The hairdresser had applied a glue-like substance, which he had called "gel". This concept was new to Uma Nath. When he looked at the mirror, he smiled. But he was not happy with his look. It was not glowing like Sunil Chauhan.

In the DAV hostel, Sunil was the new idol, and he had a girlfriend. A day ago, Tunni had come to the hostel, and every guy was jealous. Sunil was instantly famous. Now, it was Uma's turn.

Sunil had once mentioned that you need to shave against the grain of the beard to get a close green-tint look. Uma took the blade, but his hand trembled. He went to Dinesh naai, a guy who had a shop outside the campus gate.

"Don't touch my hair, just shave," Uma Pandey ordered Dinesh.

Dinesh looked at Uma with surprise. "*Uma Bhaiya, satiya gaye hain kya*? You are already shaved," said Dinesh, and he rubbed his barber knife on a sharpening stone. The screeching sound irked Uma.

"Don't use this knife. Use Gillette, and shave against the grain," Uma said.

"Why?"

"That gives a greenish tint look, and use disposable blades. This knife can give infections."

"Oh, greenish tint like Sunil?" smirked Dinesh.

This guy, Sunil, was becoming more renowned than *Guddu Bhaiya*, Uma thought. One day he may surpass Guddu's popularity.

"Sunil is a *Majnu*. Don't be like him, *Uma Bhaiya*. I have heard that he brings prostitutes to boy's hostel. If you live with him, indeed, you will get H.I.V. You are *Guddu Bhaiya's* friend. Be like him. He is a man of words. He is ferocious as a lion. Why are you following Sunil? A few weeks ago, Sunil was beaten here, at this gate with some *chokraas*. *DAV hostel ka naam kharab kar diya*, and *Guddu Bhaiya's* too."

Uma did not like Dinesh's comments. The hostel gossips spread like jungle fire. If he brought Rakshita to the hostel, the guys might think of her as a prostitute. No, he would never do that. Uma decided to follow Guddu's league. He got up from the rickety wooden chair.

"What happened, *Bhaiya*?" Dinesh asked.

"No, I'm good. I don't need that greenish look." Uma walked off.

Uma looked at the sky. It may rain. He fiddled in his pocket and checked two tickets for the matinee show. *Wo Ladki Bahot Yaad Aati Hai*, he had played this song umpteen times on his cassette player. On Zee tv, as advised by Rakshita, he had seen the trailer too. Neha Dhupia in a pink bikini was steaming hot. He had imagined Rakshita in a bikini. In his dreams, Rakshita had blazed and roasted his heart. He took his hand and placed it on the left side of his rib cage. It was thumping.

✳

Winter and sweaters are old lovers, and mothers from India start weaving this love story in September. Sumati Devi, Bechu's mother, had selected and bought yarns carefully. She wanted to ensure that her son wore the fitting lucky sweater, a pullover, for his next CA exam. She had discussed the design, patterns and colour with Rimjhim.

"Aunty, the new issue of Grihsobha has Marino yarn designs. You should try that. It will look good on Amit," Rimjhim suggested. Rimjhim preferred calling him Amit, not Bechu.

Rimjhim used to get lots of ideas about Bechu from Bechu's mother. Sumati Aunty was becoming her favourite.

"Thanks, Rimjhim, let me ask Bechu to bring Grihsobha,"

"It's okay, Auntie, let him study. I will go and get it."

"No, you don't. The shopkeeper, that magazine-wala, Gupta is a lecher," mother warned.

"Oh, really?"

"The whole day he sits at his shop and gapes at Tunni, that Rai's daughter. Some guys from the notorious DAV hostel are also after her. Can you believe she is in twelfth grade? Her mother claims that she is IIT-JEE material, but she roams around with guys at this age. She is younger than you," Sumati confirmed the rumour.

Rimjhim felt a sharp pang in her heart after hearing the name of the DAV hostel. In her last colony, she was already the subject of gossip because of Guddu Shukla. Here also, the DAV boys were active. Suddenly she wanted to have a good reputation in the eyes of Bechu's mother. Why she needed this validation, she was not sure. She thought to go and see Bechu, who was studying in the next room, but she somehow stopped herself. She imagined going to the magazine shop, skimming through some romance novels or talking about a book, but this kind of dream could not come true in a small city. She had heard a lot about Bechu through his mother. Bechu's dreams, his ambitions, his likes and dislikes, and his vulnerabilities. Bechu's dedication and commitment to become a CA attracted her more.

What she wanted to become, she was not yet sure. She had taken admission in B.A. Sanskrit just to oppose her father. She wanted to become a doctor, like any other girl. But when she talked about this to Shatrughan Singh, he advised her to take any subject she could easily pass, like home science. First, Shatrughan had discouraged her, saying that she was not meant to be a doctor. Her marks were not good enough to study medicine. Later, she heard her father telling her mother, "A girl is like a debt, so why invest money in her education? Eventually, she will get married and go to someone else's house." She took two years to decide what she wanted to study after her twelfth exams. Instead of home science, she took admission in Sanskrit, a minor act of revolt against her father. Now at the age of twenty-two, she was still a B.A. Sanskrit final year student.

✳

Someone cranked a Bollywood song on a boom box, "*Wo Ladki Bahot Yaad Aati Hai.*" Bechu cringed. This broke his concentration, and he closed his book on corporate tax.

"Who is playing this music in the late morning?!" he screamed and checked the time. It was 10:30 am.

"It must be Rakshita," Bechu heard Rimjhim's sweet voice. "Yesterday, she taped these songs into a cassette," Rimjhim said to Bechu's mother.

Bechu could not stop himself. He got to his feet and came out of his room. Bewildered by Rimjhim's voice and her presence, he saw many old *Grihsobha* and *Manorama* magazines littered on the floor. In a dandelion-yellow suit and blue bangles, Rimjhim was flipping the pages. Their eyes met again, and Bechu's heart raced. With a faint, secretive, and heartbeat-skipping smile, Rimjhim avoided looking into Bechu's eye. It is true, the best path to blossom love is through eyes. This path meets the soul at the destination. Bechu felt like a superman.

"Oh good, you are here. Can you go to Gupta's magazine stall and get the latest issue of Grihshobha?" Bechu's mother asked, breaking Bechu's reverie.

"Where is Chotu?" Bechu asked.

"It's a school day."

Bechu realized that it was still Wednesday. For him, all days were the same, like accountancy and tax laws.

"Please go – I don't want to send her to Gupta's shop. Look, she is helping me to knit a sweater for you."

Bechu got excited about the idea of the sweater. Maybe it would bring a bit of good luck to him. He had to pass this exam, and he had promised himself.

✳

Uma tried to peep through a window. He could not see anything at first, but he finally caught a glimpse when the light-cream curtains fluttered at Rakshita's house. He started and revved his bike so that Rakshita could hear it. He heard a faint sound of the song. Finally, he was going to have a date. Uma was well dressed. He had put on deodorant and was expecting the Axe effect. His shirt was well creased, fitting like a glove. He had also noted a piece of extra advice: never try to kiss a girl on the first date. These were the exact words from Sunil Chauhan. After all, after winning Tunni's heart, Sunil was treated like a God in the hostel. Though Uma never liked him, he had to listen to him.

Uma heard a creaking sound and saw a boy was coming down the stairs. His blue Hawaiian chappel made a splashing sound as if it was wet. Uma compared himself with Bechu. What a *bhikhari*-type dress-sense Bechu had. Uma smirked.

Suddenly, Uma realized that Bechu may see him and create a scene. He started his bike and drove away to Gupta's magazine stall. Rakshita might show up in a few minutes. She could walk up to the local bazaar to catch an auto. There were lines of *auto-walas* in front of Gupta's shop. Many of them kept looking up at the fourth floor to catch a glimpse of Tunni. But they were careful: the moment they saw an older person or guy from the same street coming by, they would get busy with their own chores.

Uma saw Bechu strolling towards Gupta's shop. When the *auto-walas* saw Bechu, they scurried as if they had found passengers. Gupta also got busy arranging his magazines. Scared and with a tremendous wrenching feeling in his stomach, Uma picked a magazine and hid his face.

Bechu picked a *Grihshobha* magazine and glanced through its pages. Uma could not control his amusement at the sight of Bechu Mishra reading a women's magazine.

Bechu heard Uma's titters. "What the hell are you doing here?" Bechu snarled.

"Arey, Bechu brother, how are you?" Uma asked sheepishly as if he was not sure how he had come to land in this colony. As Bechu was glaring at him, Uma ran to his bike and opened his backpack to collect a box of fresh *ladoos*.

"*Bechu Bhaiya*, have it," Uma offered.

"Why, what is the occasion?" Bechu was reluctant and confused.

"I came top in the exam," Uma tried to find some reason and blurted out.

"Again?" Bechu remembered that Uma had mentioned that he was the district topper of the year 1999, in the matriculation exam.

"No. That time, four years ago, I could not offer you anything. Now we are friends, and I may keep coming to your house as a friend, so this is just a tiny gesture," Uma said. He looked at the magazine in Bechu's hand and continued, "This one is an excellent magazine. Which article are you reading? That sex advisory column! That is awesome. I have read that by kissing a girl she cannot be pregnant."

This blew up Bechu's mind. He felt insulted and fumed with anger, "Get out of here, you moron. I know you are coming here for Rakshita. *Pel denge ek din sab majnungiri nikal jayega!*" Bechu exploded.

Uma sweated a bit. He started his bike sheepishly and drove away. It would be better to meet Rakshita directly at the Gunjan Cinema Hall. Then he realized that Guddu was his friend and Bechu's arrogance was nothing. He clenched his fist to show some courage, wheeled and came back.

"Don't feel bad, *Bechu Bhaiya.*" Bechu was stunned by Uma's courage. Uma handed the *Thaggu ke Ladoo* box to Bechu. "Give this to Rakshita and tell her that this is from me. She likes *ladoos.* And one more piece of advice: Read *Mastraam,* that will be more fun," Uma grinned and revved his bike.

Bechu was stunned. The behaviour of Uma Nath Pandey haunted him and wrenched his heart. He felt helpless. He was losing his grip. Should he go back to his old days, when he used to be a ferocious *rangbaaz* of the colony? Should he teach these guys some lesson, or, should he focus more on his studies as advised by Rishabh? He would wait for his turn.

10

Guddu Shukla picked up a bottle of Black Dog Whisky. He beckoned Lala. Today his room was clean and arranged. Lala was good at his work.

"Make a good peg, *patiyala* for the boys, *qila fateh kar ke aye hain dono*," Guddu sneered.

"You should have seen the face of Bechu Misir. It became small and red like a cherry," Uma boasted. "I got all this courage from you. We are friends of Guddu Shukla. Why should we be worried?"

"You guys are not my friends," Guddu growled.

"What?" Uma asked. Hearing the word and seeing Guddu's face, his hand trembled.

"You heard it. You guys are not my friends!"

Uma looked at Sunil. Lala handed over a glass to each and sat in the corner. Guddu took a sip and looked at Lala.

"Get a drink for yourself, Lala," Guddu commanded and looked at the glass. Its golden hue gave him a pleasant smell. He opened a trunk and drew a pistol from it. Sunil noticed. This box was Guddu's arsenal.

Guddu put the pistol on the floor and spun it.

"Do you see? This is original. Not a *desi katta*. It gives me power. I have power because I dare to tuck it in my trousers and walk with it. This is my friend," Guddu smirked.

Uma and Sunil laughed. Without making eye contact with Guddu, Lala sipped his whisky.

"Lala, you are safe from this Vinod Yadav and his men because of this pistol. Go. From now on, you are a free bird. I won't ask you to do my chores, clean my room."

Guddu finished his glass with a gulp. Then ordered, "Lala, one more." He grinned again.

Lala shrugged and followed Guddu's command. He had started feeling safe in Guddu's presence and his authority. He felt as if Guddu was his elder brother. He poured alcohol in glasses. This time, giving a glance at Guddu, and confidently, without asking, he made one for himself.

"So, we need to teach this Bechu some lesson so that he never tries to come near Rimjhim." Guddu rotated his finger on the glass rim. He took another sip.

"I have something in my mind *Bhaiya*," Sunil suggested. "I have to take revenge from him, so I have a plan."

"Why?"

"*Guddu Bhaiya*, while playing cricket, Bechu gave him a look and abused him. From that time, he has had a grudge against him," Uma said.

Guddu laughed. "Okay, tell me your scheme."

Sunil was about to tell them, then he realised that he was drunk, and this scheme may go against Guddu. He took a deep breath to control himself. He should not have blurted this out. This Meerut-wala would take his own sweet revenge without telling others.

"*Bhaiya*, you should confess your love to Rimjhim. Uma once said you never did," Sunil changed the topic.

"Yes, *Bhaiya*, you have never even told us when you first met her," Uma said.

"What are you guys asking?" said Guddu, blushing.

Sunil, Lala, and Uma had never seen Guddu blushing. Lala noticed that all the glasses were empty, and he poured the third *Patiyala* peg. This time he added soda, and no one noticed.

"Yes, *Bhaiya*, we want to know," Lala said. He came closer, inserting himself into the circle of big boys of the DAV hostel. He felt powerful too. This time he felt part of the group.

"Okay, I will tell the story. But you all have to follow Lucknow's etiquette of *khissagoi*. If someone is telling the story, you should not speak a word. But you have to grunt in between to indicate that you are listening."

They all gave supporting nods and exclamations and there was pin-drop silence.

"It happened three years ago, in 2000," Guddu continued.

✳

Ram Charan Shukla, the M.L.A. of Lucknow east, was a *bahubali* minister. The powerful one. He had such an aura that no one used to speak in his presence. Everyone used to weigh their words carefully before opening their mouth. I, Guddu Shukla, was his right hand.

The driveway of his massive bungalow was like a revolving door for Ambassador cars, with crisply clad ministers from state and central. That day he and his party members announced the list of who would get party tickets from where. After revealing the party details and inventory, all were happy. Ram Charan Shukla had a knack for politics, and he had full support and trust in me. I was a *yuva karykarta*, an unofficial youth leader of the party. But Ram Charan Shukla asked me to start with a minor. I had to cover only his constituency, Lucknow, and Kanpur. I was twenty, and after this election, he had promised me a more prominent role.

"R.C. Shukla *Zindabad, Guddu Bhaiya Zindabad,*" his men screamed, and these words gave me euphoria.

I had the responsibility to make sure the party was wining in his constituency and Kanpur *Dehat*. His younger brother, M.C. Shukla, was contending. Uttar Pradesh was full of caste politics – it still is. I reckoned the cast number, and I used my math. We had good support from the people of Kanpur and Lucknow. I travelled through each nook and corner of Kanpur *Dehat*. I shared election memorandums and the party's plan for the growth of Kanpur to its *janata*.

We were winning, but I had a lead that the opposition party may try to capture booths in some village area in Kanpur *Dehat*.

We came to know that the opposition would try to capture booth number 32, at Rajakiya Kanya Uchaya Vidyalaya. I informed about my apprehension to Netaji. In this area or booth, you can win only with guns and rifles. When Netaji, Ram Charan Shukla ordered, I took his blessings and marched towards booth number 32.

I reached the booth with more than ten men with rifles in their hands and pistols tucked in the waistline. We were wearing monkey caps or hiding our faces with a *gamchha,* a red scarf. There were no party hoardings or any slogan enchantments. It was better people could not guess who looted or captured the booth.

There was a police Jeep outside the booth, navy colour. On the side was written *UP police aapki seva main* (UP police for helping you). But it was helping us, the ruling party.

Police sub-inspector Nikesh was there. He knew me well. Seeing us, he said to the presiding officer, "These are the men of Netaji." He turned towards me, "Oh *Guddu Bhaiya*, I thought you wouldn't be able to come on time. We have not started any polling yet."

I came inside the polling booth, placed my rifle next to polling and presiding officers. They swallowed their spit.

The duty guard saw us. He had an old, rusted rifle to safeguard the booth. Seeing the shiny arms, he felt it would be better to keep quiet and let us do our work.

There was a big queue of men, women and girls waiting to vote. They were scared. All of them had turned pale. There was pin-drop silence. Most of them were aware of political violence. In the past election, many people had died. For them, silence was the better course. Everyone loves their life.

We were novices as well as different kinds of booth-capturers. I asked people to come forward. The officers marked their names, and I stood at the booth. I stamped Ram Charan Shukla's party or my party for every voter. The party sign of the flower. They had no choice. With every stamp, I whispered to voters, "Long live *Netaji*."

Then I saw a girl in the queue. She looked like a nymph, a celestial beauty. I had never seen such a beautiful girl in my life. Her glittering ear-studs and nose-ring made my heart skip a beat. I became nervous. I removed my monkey cap and walked towards her. My men suggested wearing it back to hide my identity, but I ignored them. I wanted to make sure my presence was etched in her heart forever.

Our eyes met. I felt magic. Her lips quivered, and she looked away. Maybe she was feeling shy. She swayed as if I was trying to touch her. I took her voter I.D. from her hand and read it. Rimjhim Singh. I read her address and memorized it.

"Wait, let madam vote," I said to the presiding officer.

They moved Rimjhim to the head of the queue. With her, a lady also moved forward. Probably she was her mother. She was aged and beautiful. I know all beautiful girls get their looks from their mothers.

"Come here and cast your vote," I told her gently with respect when the presiding officer completed his paperwork.

Rimjhim moved forward slowly and came near the booth. The iron ballot box was kept there in between the cardboard walls. I did not direct her to vote for R.C Shukla's party. I just watched her. I felt her smell. Her pheromones were enticing.

She marked her vote on the familiar sign. The flower. The *thak* sound soothed my heart.

"Our likings are the same," I found the commonalities between us.

And after this election, I pulled myself out of the party. I was not interested in politics. I went back to Lucknow and completed my degree in B.Sc. in chemistry. With mild difficulties, I passed the exam. But during my studies, most of the time, I would think about Rimjhim. I could not concentrate.

For her, I came to Kanpur. I knew her address, I arrived there. Kanpur Dehat. There I had met Uma, he was searching for his soulmate as well. Through him and others, I got to know that Rimjhim's family had moved to Kanpur City. I took admission at Kanpur University and moved into this hostel 2 years ago. I decided to do an MBA, but could not pass the exam. As my backup, I took admission in M.Sc. chemistry because that was my background. I knew nothing apart from politics and chemistry, though I didn't attend M.Sc. classes.

I searched for Rimjhim like a mad man for the next few months. But one day, I found her at the university campus near the Sanskrit department, Nunu Jha's one. I often waited outside Nunu Jha's class, but I had no guts to talk to her.

Here, reluctantly I became part of university politics. Some fellow students were aware of my background. They insisted and forced me as they were not happy with the current student leader, Vinod Yadav. I defeated Vinod Yadav by a considerable margin.

After the election, I got to know Rimjhim had voted for me. This cemented my hope. You vote for someone only when you love them. I decided I would pass the MBA and would go to her parents for a proposal.

✳

Guddu smiled when Uma grunted. His last grunt broke Guddu's musing. Uma's chest was swelled as Guddu had named him in his story. He had importance in Guddu's life. Uma looked at Sunil with pride.

"That's my story," Guddu said.

"*Bhaiya*, have you asked Rimjhim? I meant *Bhabhi*," Sunil corrected himself, "You must know if she likes you or not? Have you proposed to her?"

"No."

"You should," Uma said.

"No, this dating or roaming around with girls is not my game. I want to make Rimjhim my wife, not a girlfriend. I will try to get admission to an MBA college, and then after getting the job, I will propose to her," Guddu said.

Uma gulped his glass in one shot. He got to his feet.

"*Bhaiya*, let's go now," alcohol had given courage to Uma. He grabbed Guddu's hand and dragged him up.

"Where?"

"As you said, she is a Sanskrit, B.A. student. We will go to Nunu Jha's class. You sit there, join that class. Try to be her friend."

"But I am not a Sanskrit student. How can I sit in that class?" Guddu asked.

"*Guddu Bhaiya*, you are drunk, so you cannot think straight. You are a student leader of this university. You can even sit in the vice chancellor's class. Get ready. We are going." Uma looked at his watch.

"Yes, *Bhaiya*, you have to be a friend first, then try to convert that friendship into love. That's how this works. You are sitting here idle. What if Rimjhim falls in love with Bechu? You have to act fast. You have to tell her that you love her," Sunil suggested.

Guddu Shukla squinted at the window. He was silent for a few seconds; then after a deep sigh, he said, "Let's go."

Guddu reached the university campus, DAV college at green park Civil Lines. He sprang out from his Jeep wearing sunglasses and a red scarf. Out of habit, he tore a gutkha, but Sunil gestured for him not to do it. Guddu trusted Sunil Chauhan's advice.

"*Bhaiya*, the class will start soon, just go to the Sanskrit class and sit." Uma handed a book to Guddu and looked at his wristwatch.

Students swarmed in to greet their leader. Some bowed in respect, some folded their hands. Guddu scanned the book.

"What is this? This is the ninth-grade UP syllabus Sanskrit book," Guddu frowned.

"It does not matter, *Guddu Bhaiya*. No one is going to check your book. Here is a notebook, take some notes or scribble on it. I would suggest that you take some notes and share them with *Bhabhi*. This is how you can start your friendship," Uma said.

"Do you know where the classroom is?" Sunil asked.

"No, I have not followed Rimjhim for a year. She used to get scared of me, so I stopped. I cannot recall," Guddu said.

Sunil gestured to Lala to go and find the Sanskrit department. Lala did not like it. He used to get orders only from *Guddu Bhaiya*. He gave Sunil a look, but advanced.

In fifteen minutes, Lala came running, scanning the whole college.

"*Bhaiya*, you are here? Sanskrit department is in another corner. Let us go fast. The class has already started," Lala said.

✳

Nunu Jha was an old man on the verge of his retirement. He had given twenty years to Kanpur University, or you can say Chhatrapati Shahu Ji Maharaj University. Jha was from Bihar, Mithila region, where Jha used to do *Panditai*. One day, he got tired of his *yajaman*, parishioners, and he switched his job. His name was Narendra Narayan Jha. In short, it became Nana and then became Nunu, which means a kid's penis in some of the northern parts of India.

Nunu Jha wrote a sloka from Abhigyan Shakuntalam and recited it in his hoarse voice. His bald head was covered with some fine strands of hair.

Nunu Jha noticed that a five-foot-nine-inch-tall guy entered the classroom and took a seat at the back. He threw his heavy cardboard covered notebook on the bench, and it made a thudding sound. This attracted everyone's attention.

"Guddu! What are you doing here?" Nunu Jha folded his hand. His hand was hairier than this head.

"*Guruji*, I came here to attend Sanskrit class," Guddu said.

There were hardly fifteen students in the classroom. He looked at Rimjhim. She was on the second bench with some other girls. Most of the students in the class were girls. Rimjhim gaped at Guddu, then she looked straight ahead.

Her heart was thumping. She was scared. She wiped her face. Sweat made her armpit wet. She hated it.

"Sanskrit! But you are a science student, I thought," Jha said.

"*Guruji*, I'm interested in Sanskrit. It's a *dev-bhasha*. A language of gods. It will help me to talk directly with Him," Guddu looked at the ceiling and then smiled at Rimjhim.

Nunu Jha was an experienced man. He has seen almost sixty springs in his life. He knew how young men behave in their adolescence and how different hormones like testosterone make them aggressive.

"Guddu, get out of the class," Jha yelled.

The yelling nipped Guddu's heart. How could a mere professor yell at him – and in front of students too, in front of Rimjhim?

"Guruji, I respect you a lot. You also advise my family on astrology and Jyotish-shastra matters. I deserve a little respect in return," Guddu said.

Jha swallowed his spit. He knew Guddu very well. It was not a great idea to make him upset, but he had to save himself from embarrassment.

"*Guddu Ji*, could you please leave my class?" Jha said, showing little sarcasm as well as respect to Guddu. To students, he had to show that situation was in control, and to Guddu, he had to satisfy his ego.

Guddu sighed and gazed at Rimjhim. She was startled by his piercing glaring eyes. She fumbled and her pen dropped on the floor.

Guddu walked to the front and removed the blue moonstone ring that Jha had once given him to calm Guddu's mind. He placed it on the table and looked at Jha.

He pulled his sunglasses from his front shirt pocket and put them on. Then he walked out.

✳

Uma, Sunil, and Lala were waiting for Guddu. His Jeep was parked in front of the faculty building. A security guard came to inform them that the Jeep was parked in the wrong location, but he recognised the Jeep. It was Guddu's. He just ignored the guys who were sitting inside.

"Sunil, you told me never to try to kiss a girl on the first date. When should I kiss, then?" Uma asked.

"Why are you so eager to kiss Rakshita? Just go with the flow. Look for the signs," Sunil said.

"And what are the signs?"

"I don't know. You will get it with experience. Girls are mysterious, and everyone is different." Sunil had no idea what to say next. There was no clear and perfect answer. "How was the movie?" Sunil asked.

"It was good, we went to Gunjan Cinema. I did not like it. It was a matinee show, and people were ogling at her. She was also wearing a white deep-neck *kurti* and a blue scalloped net dupatta. I hated it when people were looking at her." Uma shrugged.

"Oh, so possessiveness is already creeping in. How come you know it was a scalloped net dupatta? When did you become such a master about girls' attire?"

"She only told me when I objected that she should not wear such revealing clothes. She got mad," said Uma.

Of course, she would have got mad, Sunil thought. She must have worn the dress to impress him, to make him proud that such a good-looking girl was with him. Sometimes, guys don't get why women dress the way they do. Men get concerned about their ladies for the lustful gazes they attract. By primitive nature, men are protective. Sunil did not want to educate Uma. A cat should not teach every lesson to a lion. But he enjoyed learning how this bunch of *Kanpuriyas* were dumb in matters of the heart.

"Next time, don't go to such theatres. There is a multiplex at Rave 3 Mall. Go there. Buy gold seats and watch a movie."

Uma did not say anything further. Already he had had to arrange money for *ladoos* and movie tickets. The mall would be an expensive treat. For a multiplex, he'd have to flick some hundreds of rupees of notes from his father's wallet.

"Will you do something for me?" asked Sunil.

"What is that?"

"Next time when you are at Gupta's shop, just inform that every Thursday, Tunni and I meet at Bitoor Ghat.

They saw Guddu Shukla coming out through an arch corridor of a rickety red building. Guddu strode towards his Jeep.

❋

"What happened? You came a little early. Did the class get dismissed?" said Uma hastily.

"That oldie is pretty mad and rude. His days are numbered. He tossed me out of the class," Guddu said irritably.

"How can he do that? *Bench ka patta nikla ke maarna tha budheey ko.* You should have taught him a lesson," said Uma.

"My *Lucknowiyat* is still intact," Guddu growled and stared at Uma. "I respect old people. He did the right thing."

Uma did not like the comment on Lucknowiyat. People from Lucknow cannot even drink the water of Gomti, but still, they carry the attitude. They think they are more sophisticated than *Kanpuriyas*.

"Fine, so what is next?"

"Nothing, let's go back to the hostel. I cannot do this friendship thing, if you love someone you cannot be friends," said Guddu.

"*Bhaiya*, I would advise you to propose," said Sunil. Like a wise man, he chewed his words. "From Tunni, I have heard that the friendship between Bechu and Rimjhim is growing. You have to act, to get out ahead of Bechu."

"Let's go to the hostel and discuss it. I will do this in the upcoming days," Guddu said as he started his Jeep.

The next few days, in DAV boys hostel room number 21, Uma, Sunil and Lala plotted how Guddu should propose Rimjhim on Tuesday. They came up with multiple ideas from Bollywood movies, from *Mohabbatin* to films of the nineties, from SRK to Ajay Devgan.

Everyone had their own choice. Lala was a Mithun Chakraborty fan. He advised either to dance like a Mithun's disco dancer or Julie-Julie song. Everyone laughed. Dancing around trees happens only in the movies. When his dancing idea was rejected, he advised writing some heart-melting words on maple leaves. But where to find maple in Kanpur. It was the fall season, but Kanpur was not the right place.

Uma, as usual, went with Chunky Pandey. But for him also, it was hard to recollect romantic songs of Pandey. Most of them were from the eighties with Neelam. Nothing was iconic with Chunky Pandey. Then he recalled that Rakshita and Rimjhim both liked Ajay Devgan.

"*Bhaiya*, why don't you do a leg-split scene like Ajay Devgan? You can make an entry to DAV college like him, in front of *Bhabhi*. Then roll down and give her a rose, as you are sitting on your knees," Uma said excitedly. His eyes glittered like a child's.

"Can you guys stop this indiyapa? I want it simple," Guddu shouted.

Guddu noticed a bleached streak in Uma's front hair. "And what the hell is that?" asked Guddu, pointing at Uma's head.

"Oh, that's Ajay Devgan style. Have you seen *Pyaar To Hona Hi Tha*?"

It was clear to Guddu and Sunil that Uma was in love. He was changing his habit and his dress-sense, inspired by Sunil. If someone is changing in a good direction, he should not be judged. Guddu decided not to comment further.

"*Bhaiya*, I have some advice," Sunil muttered.

"*Bako be*, you are full of advice," said Guddu.

"This Tuesday, propose in Bechu's colony. An enemy should be tormented. *Uskey chaati pe saanp lotna chahiye*," said Sunil approaching his point with slow relish, "Think about the reaction, when he comes to know that you had proposed to Rimjhim on his own turf!"

It was the second Tuesday of September 2003. Autumn was knocking on the door of Kanpur's weather, asking the monsoon to end. On this pleasant, overcast Kanpur afternoon, Rimjhim left her classroom. Looking at the black clouds, she felt it could rain in the next few hours. She drew her books closer to her chest. Nervously, she looked around and did not find any trace of Guddu. She took a deep breath.

For the past few weeks, she had been feeling alone. Rakshita was busy either watching movies or meeting Uma Nath. Rakshita had started trying new dresses, waxing her arms, and applying new kinds of makeup creams, which irked Rimjhim more. Rimjhim wanted to do the same, but for whom?

She did not know Guddu well. She had not spoken to him. Whenever she used to see Guddu, fear used to travel within her from head to toe. She had first seen him during the last UP election. She was voting for the first time. From that day onward, Guddu entered her life, and her world turned upside down.

Now she had met Bechu. She liked him but was not sure whether Bechu liked her or not. Bechu wanted something else in life. He was desperate to pass an exam she had never heard of before. It must be a tough one.

Further, she is twenty-two years old now. Bechu was a year younger and an inch shorter than her. But who cared? The wise men's adage is true; love is blind. It does not see age or height. Anyways, she never liked high heels.

Rimjhim hailed an auto for Barra. It began to drizzle near Civil Lines. From Civil Lines to Barra, it took around thirty minutes in traffic.

✳

When Rimjhim's auto approached her house, she saw two familiar faces and a few boys. She recognised Guddu and Uma, but not the other two guys.

Guddu's Jeep was parked in front of Bechu's iron gate. Her heart took a jolt. She asked the auto-wala not to stop, and to keep driving. She did not want drama in front of her new rented home. She had already suffered from the last fiasco.

She looked back and saw Guddu's Jeep following. He might have noticed her. She had to face it. She had also read some news about how unrequited lovers of UP react. Some of them threw acid. With this horrible thought, she asked the auto-wala to stop near the bazaar, which was a little crowded. If something happened, she might get some support from the crowd.

With trembling hands, she drew money from her purse. Using the other hand, she clutched her books hard. She glanced to her right. Guddu brought his Jeep to a stop a few yards away and jumped out. He stormed towards her. Surprisingly, the auto-wala passed a salaam to Guddu and scurried away.

Rimjhim scrutinised Guddu's hand. There were no bottles, blades or any dangerous weapon. She breathed a sigh of relief, but this vanished when she noticed a red rose. It was sharper than any blade.

"*Hum aapsey bahut prem kartey hain*," Guddu blurted out. He bent and tried to kneel, but he was reluctant and embarrassed to pull off this act in public.

Rimjhim drew her confidence back. At least Guddu did not look threatening. Traffic stopped to take a glimpse, and onlookers turned, gaping and gawking at them.

"Guddu, leave. I want to go home," Rimjhim looked straight at the rickety gate of her house, which was a few furlongs away.

"I will make you happy. *Khus rakhengey hum aapko*," said Guddu, holding Rimjhim's hand.

Rimjhim silently sobbed. There was now no breath of wind stirring. She felt like someone was gnawing her gut. A teardrop seeped through her eyes when she noticed the staring crowd. No one spoke a word. With humiliation, she tried to twist her hand to draw herself from Guddu's grip.

"Why don't you understand my feelings? I breathe for you... Each second, I think of you," said Guddu, letting go of her hand, but a sense of desire and conquest gripped Guddu's heart. He grabbed it back, "Always remember, I'm not scared of anyone. One day you will be married to me," Guddu gazed into her eyes.

Then with arrogance, Guddu turned away and walked off. He jumped in his Jeep and drove away.

The first shower began to fall from the overcast sky. Rimjhim stood still. She could see the gate but could not walk a step. She felt so helpless that she could die of shame. She could not talk about this to her father. He would blame her.

That was what he always did. Instead of trying to solve the problem, he would blame people for bringing the pain. In fear of getting drenched, people scurried away to hide. With a heavy heart, Rimjhim took the first step towards her house. She noticed Bhujang standing dumbfounded in the corner. She trudged along as fast as she could.

＊

Bechu's books fluttered with the cold breeze that was coming with driving rain and squall. He pushed his chair and reached out to the window to close it. He saw Rimjhim on the street. She was strolling towards the house without any umbrella.

Bechu grabbed an umbrella and ran downstairs. He opened the gate and walked towards her. When she saw Bechu, she smiled. She forgot her pain. Reluctantly Bechu offered the umbrella, which Rimjhim accepted, though she was drenched.

"It looks like *Singh Saheb* never forced you to study science," said Bechu, looking at the wet Sanskrit book in Rimjhim's hand.

This was the first time Rimjhim did not feel bad at a nasty comment about her educational background.

"I'm studying it by my choice. I wanted to study Sanskrit."

"Good choice. It has good scope," said Bechu flatly.

Rimjhim looked at Bechu. She was astonished. For the first time in her life, someone was telling her that Sanskrit had good scope. Till now, everyone used to make fun of her. Till now, even she was clueless about what career scope Sanskrit had.

"How?" Rimjhim asked curiously.

"Well, you can do an M.A. at Delhi University. After that, you can try to become a lecturer. Many Sanskrit literature books are not available in Hindi and English for the common masses. You can translate them. You can also join a foreign university."

"Oh, I never thought about that."

Bechu smiled. Within a second, Rimjhim had forgotten all the humiliation that she had endured because of Guddu. In Bechu's eyes, she saw hope. A positivity, which was something very few people had bestowed in her life.

"Think about it. You could be an outstanding Sanskrit scholar of D.U. or JNU. You could be a professor emeritus by the age of sixty. The best-looking professor emeritus of any university," said Bechu while folding his umbrella, entering the front yard.

"Definitely," smiled Rimjhim. She felt like it was her best day. She had found her own goal in life. Now she knew why she was studying Sanskrit. With new hope, the sun gleamed out of ragged clouds. The rain lessened.

The next few days passed quickly. The CAT and other MBA exam forms were out, and Guddu got busy with filling out forms and his preparations. He loathed the idea of proposing Rimjhim. It had been a big mistake, but there was no need to apologise. He had never apologised to anyone in his life.

Uma met with Rakshita at Rave 3 Mall. This time he watched the movie at a multiplex, but the ticket was so expensive that he spent the entire time thinking about the price. The idea of kissing Rakshita did not occur, and he tried to touch her, making it look like random strokes. Uma was a chicken who never showed the courage to be with a girl. Tired of waiting, Rakshita grabbed his hand and held it in her lap. Uma liked the warmth and sensation more than the song *"Tauba Tumhare Yeh Ishare"* of the movie Chalte Chalte.

After the movie, they strolled through a bookstore. Uma had seen magazines at Gupta's store, but books or magazines never attracted him. A magazine's heading caught his eyes. It was *Cosmopolitan*: "12 magical sentences to whisper while kissing a girl." Secretly, Uma purchased the book.

✳

Bhujang had stopped going to Gupta's store. Catching a glimpse of Tunni was a pain these days. He felt alone. Everyone was busy chasing their goal. He thought of asking for money from his father to buy some equipment for his dream gym but never had the courage. The possibility of his father asking him for a degree or his plans, which he had avoided for the past two years, held him back. He had lied that he had taken admission in B.A. History. He had failed the twelfth grade, but his cybercafé friend had printed a fake mark sheet showing that he had passed.

He should have studied well. If that was the case, he would have been able to impress Tunni with his stylish English. The way Sunil spoke...

Eventually, his threads of thoughts were back to Tunni. He was surprised at how obsessed he had become. One last time, he wanted to check with Gupta or Afzal about Tunni. How Tunni was doing. She was the petite and perfect example of the Bihari's couplet *'Dekhan Main Chote Laage, Ghaav Kare Gambhir.'*

With a *"gambhir ghaav"* of her on his mind, he marched to Barra Bazar, a few minutes' walk from his home.

He was surprised to see the deserted front of Gupta's shop or Tunni's house. There were no auto-walas to deal with. He smiled. Now he had to exert less effort to chase them away. Or maybe last time when he scolded them, they all got scared.

"Oh, *Bhujang Bhaiya*, seeing you after a long time," Gupta sneered.

"No Gupta, last week only. When *Guddu Bhaiya* made his presence felt at Barra Bazar, Bhujang was there, he was standing at the corner," Afzal said. Afzal's tone and hand gestures made clear that he was impressed by Guddu.

"Are you also preparing for some exam like Bechu? He is so engrossed that he does not even care that other guys are knocking and challenging his authority in Barra," Gupta added.

"Can you stop talking nonsense about *Bechu Bhaiya*? Let him just get through his exam in November, then you will not see these *tuchhas* here in our colony."

"Leave *Bechu Bhaiya*, what about you? I have heard that your Tunni meets that *Meeruth-wala* every Thursday at 3:00 in Bithoor, near Ganga. I have heard that Sunil picks her up from Chemistry tuition, and they meet there," Afzal added. He folded the fingers of both hands like a bird's beak and then brought them together. "*Bithoor pata hai na, laundey lafaadey choche ladane jaate hain.*"

This boiled Bhujang's blood. He grabbed Afzal's collar and slapped him. Gupta came running.

"*Dengey kantaap jyada backchodi kiya tho*. Tunni is a nice girl."

"Why the hell are you taking out your frustration on him? If you don't believe, go to Bithoor on Thursday at 3:00 and see for yourself," said Gupta.

"Okay, you two have to come with me and lend your bike," said Bhujang.

*

Tunni and Sunil walked to the steps of Patthar Ghat. It was quiet, and they sat together, clung to each other. Tunni held Sunil's hand tightly.

This was their third meeting here, and every time Sunil waited for Bhujang patiently. Initially, he was mainly interested in making Bhujang jealous, but later he started liking Tunni. For hours and hours, Tunni talked about her family, her younger brother, and her plans to clear IIT and visit different places in the US.

"My *Bua* lives in New York. My *fufu* works there in IT. One day after my engineering degree, I will also go there," said Tunni.

"So, you are going to dump me?"

"No, you can also come, get admission there in NYU. Do MS and try to get a job."

"I don't have enough money to do masters in the US."

"Then take a job here, in Noida, there are a lot of BPO companies. After some experience, they transfer them to the US. My *fufu* got transferred like that. On H1B visa."

For a moment, Sunil considered Tunni's *fufu* an enemy. He hated the man he had never seen. Why do some girls love their *jijaji* or *fufu* more than anybody in the world? These were third-world problems that could not be solved.

"I want to join the Indian Army. They don't transfer," said Sunil

"Oh, let's not think about it. We have plenty of time, almost five years to ponder," Tunni deflected the topic. Her earring glittered in the sun's rays. Sunil's heart raced. Why the hell did Uma rank her at number three? Sunil finally had gotten a glimpse of Rimjhim. She was like an ordinary girl. She was just fair, like a cow. Well, Sunil accepted Rimjhim was beautiful, but nothing compared to Tunni. Tunni could be more attractive if … With this thought, Sunil reached into his pocket for something.

"I have something for you."

"What is that?" Tunni snatched the packet from Sunil's hand. She opened it. She got excited. "A nose ring," Tunni gasped.

"You did not like it?"

"No, it's beautiful. I wanted one. See, my nose is pierced," Tunni showed him. She removed the screw and placed it in her nose. "How does this look?"

"Oh, breath-taking. You have been moved from number three to number one."

"Just breath-taking? And who was at number one before?"

"Nothing. I meant, Sania Mirza is the number one Indian tennis player, and you look better than her in this nose ring."

Tunni blushed, and for a few seconds, Sunil beheld her beauty. "Can I kiss your nose?"

"What? Who desires to kiss a nose?" Tunni blushed.

"I want to kiss your nose."

"No, you will try to kiss my lips. It's not allowed."

"Promise, not even the nose. I just want to kiss my gift, that ring."

"Okay, kiss it." With a secretive and playful smile, Tunni started removing the ring to give it to Sunil.

Sunil grabbed her hand and kissed her. Tunni did not protest. Sunil moved ahead and kissed her nose ring. Tunni's lips parted. She waited for Sunil to take charge and taste her.

Reading the moment, Sunil grabbed her tightly. Her touch was like a spark. Sunil next kissed her cheek and then lips.

"This is wrong," Tunni said, but her hand reached for Sunil's shirt button.

Sunil slid his hand in her *kurti* and kissed her again to stop her from protesting. Tunni shivered, and she responded with another kiss, outdoing Sunil in her ardour.

"I love you, Tunni," Sunil whispered in her ear and stroked her soft breast.

"Stop talking. You talk too much and call me Khushi," Tunni hushed him, pushing him back gently. She kissed him passionately and nibbled his lower lip.

✳

"*Sala bahenchod,*" Sunil heard someone bellow, just before he was pulled into the air. Tunni screamed. One more guy grabbed Sunil's leg.

"Bhujang, please leave us alone!" pleaded Tunni.

Bhujang glared at her with bulging red eyes. Gupta and Afzal grabbed Sunil's legs and hands. Bhujang punched Sunil in the stomach. Sunil writhed on the floor and spat up blood.

"Let's go to Barra. I will show *Rai Ji* what kind of IIT-JEE preparation his daughter is doing. *Yehi gul khila rahi hai saali,*" Bhujang snarled. A stream of tears fell from his eyes. "I loved you more than any guy could have." He looked at Tunni.

"Leave him alone. Please don't hit him so hard!"

Two *pandits* from the nearby temple of the Ghat came running, and a few visitors joined them.

"Don't dare to get involved in my family matters. This roadside Romeo was eve-teasing my sister," Bhujang warned them.

Sunil and Tunni looked at Bhujang with surprise.

"*Kyun? Kewal tum hi harami ho sakte ho*, I'm an equally good player," Bhujang whispered in Sunil's ear. He grabbed Tunni's hand and pulled her. "Let's go back home," he snarled. "Leave him to enjoy Ganga's water and evening rituals."

Sunil looked at Tunni. She was trying to escape. Sunil could not breathe, and his vision was blurred. Tunni's yellow *salwar-kameez* disappeared into the yellowish and orange hue of the Ganga sunset.

Bechu never got the lyrics of English songs. Many times, he tried really hard to understand what the singer was saying. After lengthy efforts, he could only catch the first line of the Robbie Williams song: "I will talk, and Hollywood will listen." But he felt it sounded better than "*Wo ladka bahut yaad aata hai.*" Rakshita had played this song so many times that Bechu hated it. In fact, he had started hating Ajay Devgan.

"Why do you listen to such English songs?" said Bechu. "Do you get the meanings? I have to read the cassette cover to understand the lyrics."

"This song is about hope. You should see Robbie William's expressions, his attitude, his stance when he sings. The video comes on MTV," said Rishabh. He brought their ritual cup of tea, which Bechu always demanded.

"Why do you consider your life is hopeless?" said Bechu, staring into Rishabh's eyes.

"Did you see the admit card? My exam centre is Vidya Mandir Mahila Mahavidyalaya, What's yours?" Rishabh deflected the question.

"It's always Vidya Mandir."

"Rishabh, are you hiding something? Is there something you want to share?" asked Bechu.

"No."

"Then why do you listen to such gloomy songs, read self-help books or try to escape in literature? Are you happy?"

"Who says people who escape in literature are not happy? Why do you guys perceive us like this?" Rishabh snapped. "Have you checked the schedule?"

"Again, you are changing the topic. I have noticed you always call me home when auntie is not around. It has been three years of our friendship. I have never met her."

"She has gone to Delhi for office work. Now, tell me, have you checked the schedule? You are appearing in both groups, right?"

"Yes, the first group in the first week of November and the second group in the second week of November," Bechu said. He gave up asking further questions. He knew Rishabh would not say a word, as he had never opened up.

Bechu looked at himself in a mirror. He smiled, and he hummed a few lines of Robbie Williams songs. Rishabh was amazed. A few seconds ago, Bechu was worried about him and his agony, and now he was smiling.

"Can I say something in crude *Kanpuriya* dialect?" Rishabh asked.

"Yeah."

"There is a saying in Hindi, '*hum udti chidiya ke choch ka rang dekh ke bata sakte hain*'," Rishabh smirked.

"What do you mean? And your phrase is wrong, it's something else."

"You are in love," said Rishabh. "Why don't you propose to her?"

"You know what? Bhujang is correct. You are too inexperienced and gentlemanly to be a *Kanpuriya*." Bechu thought for a while. There was a weird silence in the room. "I'm not going to tell her."

"Life – or love – is not a Bollywood movie. If you like her, you have to tell her."

"I have learnt love lessons from Hindi movies, and if my love is pure, then one day I will get married to her," Bechu said in a dramatic way. "You never fell in love?"

"No."

"Why, you never liked anyone?"

"I've never found someone of my type."

"Then what's your type?" Bechu asked.

"Can you concentrate? We are here for combined studies and to analyse the past ten years' questions of group one."

This was Rishabh. He was always good at deflecting questions about himself, but he was excellent at forcing people to confide in him.

✳

It was the first week of October, and Guddu was sweating. He looked at the Durga poster that he had placed for Navratri. He prayed and started checking answers to the English MBA test series, the self-test series he had bought on Uma's advice.

He matched his answers with the series, and most of them were wrong. He cringed. His final score was four out of fifty. In frustration, he threw his pencil. He never hated verbal reasoning and English comprehension this much before.

He picked up a book, *Word Power Made Easy*, of which he had never read more than four pages. It was the most tedious and mundane book in the world.

He heard the familiar sound of a Bajaj Pulsar bike. It must be Sunil. He had been away from the hostel for weeks, and Guddu closed the book when Sunil barged in.

"I have told you always knock on the door," Guddu bellowed. He noticed the bruises and Sunil's blackened eye. "*Aa gaye phir se laat kha ke*? Now don't say that Bechu's men have beaten you again?"

Sunil lowered his gaze. He crimped the courage to speak further. "*Bhaiya Tunni ko hum pataye hain.* She likes me too."

"Shut your gob. If you love someone, never use the word *pataana*. If you love the girl, then respect the girl." Guddu hesitated a bit. It reminded him how he had behaved with Rimjhim a few weeks ago at Barra Bazar.

"Sorry, *Guddu Bhaiya*," Sunil's voice choked.

"Do you see the paper on the table? That is the CAT admit card. Now you tell me, should I prepare for the exam or solve your love triangle? I know I don't have even a slim chance for IIM, but at least I want a decent MBA college. So that I can become an investment banker."

"*Bhaiya*, you guessed it right, it was Bechu's man... Bhujang," interrupted Uma. He was standing at the door.

"*Bhaiya*, he mishandled Tunni. He abused her and slapped her. He went back and told Tunni's father that we were snogging. Now her parents are not letting her go out, not even for her IIT-JEE preparation coaching," said Sunil in a brittle voice.

Guddu's face turned maroon when he heard Bechu's name.

"*Sala*, I have been trying hard to concentrate on my MBA. The exam is on 23rd November and *yeh Bechu ka aadmi kand kar ke laal kiye jaa raha hai meri.* Now I will turn them red."

Guddu picked up his Jeep's keys. Silently, Uma, Sunil and Lala followed.

✳

Kanpur's Barra Bazar Road was dusty even in October. Dust could be found in any season or any month. Gupta drew out a duster to dust off the magazines. He saw Guddu across the street. Like a rocket, he shut down the shop shutter and flew away on his bike.

Sunil, with his limping leg, caught Afzal, who had noticed them too late. His heart sank, and his voice choked when he saw Guddu Shukla. Sunil dragged him to the Jeep.

"*Guddu Bhaiya. Kasam se*, it was Bhujang. I did not even touch Tunni," Afzal bleated. He was aware that if he did not tell the truth, the goat would be *halaled* today.

"Go and bring Bhujang, I'm waiting here." Guddu held Afzal's cheek with both hands and gazed into his eyes. Afzal followed it as the supreme commandment. "Wait, we will follow you, *aaj ghar se ghaseet ke marengey*." Guddu jumped from the driver's seat.

Guddu beckoned Lala. Lala followed Guddu's gesture and lifted the big black Tawa and kerosene stove from Afzal's *chat khomcha*, a small vendor's cart on bamboo sticks.

Afzal begged in disbelief as Lala placed that Tawa and stove on the Jeep's back seat. "That is my bread and butter. *Guddu Bhaiya*, please don't break it."

"Just do what we tell you."

Afzal slithered through various narrow gullies of Barra. After walking for some twenty minutes, they reached the door of an old rickety house. The green paint on the door was peeling off, and when Afzal knocked on it, a speck of green and brown dust flew off.

Bhujang opened the door. "What's the matter, Afzal?" he asked, then he saw that Guddu, Uma, Lala and Sunil appeared in front of him. Bhujang tried to close the door, but the four men overpowered him. They kicked him in the stomach, and when Bhujang started writhing on the floor, Uma and Sunil tied Bhujang's legs and hands.

"*Rakh sale ko Jeep main*. Load the bastard into the Jeep," bellowed Guddu.

A few courageous guys from Barra tried to intervene, but when they saw a pistol tucked in Guddu's waistline, they kept quiet and scurried away. The bullet was mightier than any standard bravado.

Lala and Uma pushed Bhujang into the back seat. He tried to scream and wriggle. But as his mouth was also strapped, only a whimpering sound was coming out of it.

"Afzal, hop on and hold your Tawa securely," Guddu said while starting his Jeep. "Where was the place where all this shit happened? I meant where he fought with you," Guddu asked Sunil.

"*Bhaiya*, Patthar Ghat, Bithoor," said Sunil.

Patthar Ghat at Ganga was deserted at noon. Afzal put the black cast iron *tava* on the kerosene stove. He pumped the kerosine stove for a while and set it on fire. Orange and blue flame swirled with a buzzing sound.

Bhujang was sitting in the corner, wondering what would happen next. He felt scandalised. He was at the place where a few weeks ago he had beaten Sunil, and now it was his turn. But instead of slapping or knocking him down, Sunil and Guddu were planning to cook something.

Guddu tore a packet of *gutkha* and poured it into his mouth. He flicked the packet in his peculiar style.

"Lala, check if the *tava* is hot or not," he said, as he handed one more *gutkha* packet to Lala.

Lala smiled, and also poured *gutkha* into his mouth. After chomping and chewing it for a minute, Lala spat it on the *tava*. The red *gutkha* spittle sizzled and turned black. Lala gave a look of triumph to Guddu.

"Remove the straps," said Guddu to Sunil. Sunil followed.

"*Guddu Bhaiya*, please. I will not show my face to you guys ever again," cried Bhujang.

"Sunil, have you tried bottom fry?" Guddu asked Sunil, ignoring Bhujang's pleading. He sat on the stairs and looked at the Ganga River. Guddu felt calm and surreal.

"No *Bhaiya*," replied Sunil.

"Then fry it."

Sunil and Uma pulled Bhujang. He was heavy. Bhujang wriggled hard. Sunil beckoned to Afzal for help.

"Afzal, no! We are friends! Save me Afzal," Bhujang screamed.

"Wait, don't drag him. Cut the straps from his legs and hands."

Hardly daring to breathe, Afzal crouched and cut the straps.

"Bhujang, sit on the *tava*," Guddu glared at him.

"*Bhaiya, galti ho gayi*. I made a mistake," Bhujang whimpered.

"Sit on it," Guddu repeated, without displaying any emotion.

Bhujang removed his trousers. He sat on the *tava*. His buttocks sizzled, and he howled. The pain was like piercing thousands of swords through his rear. He screamed till his voice left his body. The smell of burning flesh crept into Afzal's nostrils.

Bhujang jumped in pain. He fell to the ground and wriggled as if someone had poured a pinch of salt on an earthworm.

"*Tarbooz sik gaya.* The watermelon has been roasted," Uma laughed.

Guddu came close to Bhujang to make sure he could hear him clearly. "Never try to create a brawl with my boys. These skirmishes will be expensive for you. Now you have paid the price. But remember, this time, I baked your bottom. Next time it will be your front. You won't be able to make love," said Guddu. He looked at Afzal, "You, make *chaat-chola* on the same *tava* and offer it to Bechu. I hope he will find it tasty. Tell him that it's from my side. And take this guy to the hospital. Tell the doctors that it was an accident," Guddu ordered Afzal.

✳

Bechu reached the gate of Hallet Hospital at Swaroop Nagar. After coming out from the auto, he looked around for Rishabh. He had called him because it was easy for Rishabh to reach there, Rishabh's house being just a few minutes away.

"Why did you call me to Hallet hospital?" asked Rishabh.

"Bhujang has been admitted," Bechu said hastily as he paid the auto-wala. He knew that if he had told Rishabh over the phone about Bhujang, Rishabh might not have come to meet him.

"What happened to him? Did he hurt himself in the gym?"

"No, I don't know yet. But I know he was found unconscious at Patthar Ghat. Some *pujaris* of nearby temples brought him here."

"Patthar Ghat, near Bithoor? What the hell was he doing there?"

"How do I know? Let's go, common ward. His bed number is 42."

Bechu had lied to Rishabh. He felt uneasy. He had never lied to him before, but he did not want to tell everyone about Afzal and his visit.

Bechu and Rishabh reached the corridor. There was no security, and meeting tokens were not required to meet the patient. Rishabh just followed Bechu. He thought about asking how Bechu was aware of the room number in the hospital but did not care to investigate.

They saw a short, stout man in the corridor, and a funny-looking guy was walking a foot behind. He was in a see-through shirt with bleached hair. They gazed at Bechu as if they both knew him.

"Who are these guys?" asked Rishabh.

"I don't know them, but they look familiar," said Bechu.

"I think I have seen them before."

Bechu and Rishabh entered the general ward. There were multiple beds. Different patients squeaked or writhed on the bed.

Rishabh scanned the beds. One guy's hand was severely injured. Maybe the *desi katta* had burnt his hand. Another's face was covered with white bandages. He looked like an Egyptian mummy. A case of mouth cancer because of overeating gutkha, Rishabh guessed.

After a few minutes of walking, Rishabh saw a hulky guy on a white rickety iron bed. His waistline was strapped heavily with bandages. It was easy to find Bhujang without looking for bed numbers. Standing beside him was a nurse preparing an injection. She was in a brown sari but wearing a blue coat. Real government hospital nurses were very different from movie nurses. If you see them, all your fantasies of nurse-patient romance, as shown in Hollywood movies, die instantly.

"How did this happen?" asked Bechu.

The nurse looked at Bechu. She indicated him to keep quiet and wiped Bhujang's arm with alcohol. She injected the medicine that she was preparing. Bhujang hissed like a child.

"He is over the worst of it, but for a few days, he will face trouble during motion," said the nurse.

"Motion?" asked Bechu.

"Yes, I mean when nature calls, he will feel severe pain for a few months."

Bhujang looked at Bechu and Rishabh. Rishabh said a cold "Hi," which Bhujang ignored.

"Who did this?" asked Bechu. He knew it was Guddu, but he wanted to hear the story from Bhujang, not Afzal.

"It should not matter to you. You have some educated friend," Bhujang looked at Rishabh. "Now because of these educated fake friends, you have forgotten your real friend."

"We have lots of work other than indulging in your love triangle," Rishabh roared in frustration. He was sick of being the target of Bhujang's rants.

"Yes. You won't care if our colony girls roam around with other guys. Your love is gone, so now you don't care," said Bhujang.

"Shut up!" Rishabh pointed a finger and warned him. His eyes were red and bulging with a wave of anger.

"Can you guys stop fighting?" Bechu mediated again. "Bhujang, can you tell me the whole story."

"*Tumhari wali kaa aashiq.* Lover of Rimjhim," Bhujang looked into Bechu's eyes. He glared to provoke him, taunting him to make him angry and take an action.

"Guddu Shukla?" Bechu asked to confirm.

Bhujang nodded. He was still gazing into Bechu's eyes. Bechu felt like he was getting weak, and he felt a pain in his heart which was pumping lava to his nerves.

"Bechu, we can handle this after the exam," said Rishabh.

"He stalks Rimjhim from DAV college till your house." Bhujang made sure that Bechu was listening. "In Barra Bazar, he grabbed her hand and misbehaved."

Bechu gazed at the floor. He tried to control himself.

"If you won't help, I have people to help me. Vinod Yadav and his men visited me and offered me their help."

"Who is Vinod Yadav? I have heard his name. Is this the same guy, the ex-university leader?" asked Bechu.

"Yes, he left a few minutes ago. His boys chased us from the hostel. Do you remember? When we were beating Sunil?"

"Oh, that is why their faces were familiar," Rishabh muttered.

"You don't have to ask for help from others. Your childhood friend is there. *Tu laundey ikkatha kar,* I will make sure that I'm ending this love story," Bechu snarled, and his nostril quivered.

Bhujang's lips moved to smile, but pain shuddered through his spine. He gave a winning glance to Rishabh.

"Get well soon," said Rishabh.

✸

Outside the hospital, Bechu strode so fast that Rishabh had to run to catch him. Rishabh took a handkerchief from his hand and wiped his forehead.

"This is utter stupidity."

"Cut the crap, let me decide what is stupid and what is an intelligent act," Bechu snapped. "Earlier, Bhujang was saying something."

"About what?"

"Your love is gone, so you don't care. Who was your love? What is it that he knows but I don't?" said Bechu. He was furious, and he felt that he knew nothing about his friend. If your friend wants to hide something from you, it's painful. You feel like you are not worthy of this friendship.

"You know Bhujang, most of the time he talks nonsense. That guy does not have an aim in life, and all he talks about is either Tunni or other gossip. There, back in the ward, he was clearly trying to provoke you. That, too, for his own benefit. What do you *Kanpuriyas* say? *Backchod*. He is a classic example of a *backchod*."

"See, don't ever try to hide anything from me. I don't like it."

"I have nothing to hide."

Bechu beckoned for an auto. It came and stopped.

"I'm going to talk to Afzal to arrange some boys from Chamanganj."

"Why are you doing this, Bechu? Just focus on the exam. Just one and half months and then we can take a fight with all of Kanpur."

"That Guy, he is from Lucknow and he's now challenging a *Kanpuriya. Saanp ke bil main haath daal raha hai wo.*"

"How does it matter? Why are you taking it personally?"

"You won't understand. You are from Delhi. You are not even *purabiya*."

"Yeah, I won't get it," Rishabh sighed. "I know you are doing it for your new tenant. A few months ago, you did not know her, and you had never heard her name. Before this, many guys might have eve-teased her, might have whistled at her. *Sab ka theka le rakha hai kya tumne?* With how many boys will you take revenge?"

"Now I know her. Don't ever talk like that. Sometimes, you sound very selfish. And I'm doing this for Bhujang, not for Rimjhim."

"I know you love her."

"Yes, I do. And as a friend, you have to be with me. Standing alongside, and fight with me."

"Okay fine, I will be with you. But answer me. Do you love her? Does she reciprocate your advances?" asked Rishabh with no pretence of warmth.

"It does not matter, Rishabh. You won't get it," said Bechu indifferently, gesturing to the auto-wala to start. "Barra Bazar."

The next few days Bechu spent planning to overpower Guddu Shukla and his boys. He had asked for help from Afzal, the street food vendor. Bhujang was back from the hospital, but he had been asked to take rest. Raging with revenge, he ignored the doctor's advice of bed rest and was helping Bechu to recruit people. They were preparing for a war against the DAV hostel.

When Durga Puja was in full swing at Azad Maidan, used for a *pandaal*, Bhujang reached out to the boys who played cricket with him. Bhujang had used Tunni's name, as he was aware that most of them were her admirers.

"But nowadays, we cannot see her on the terrace, and she does not come there," a lean guy named Deemak said. He took a gutkha from his pocket. Seeing this, more guys followed him. For *Kanpuriya*, Paan Masala is also a weapon. All of them had their own brand in their arsenal; Kamla Pasand, Tiranga, Pan Pasand, Pan Bahaar, Manikchand, you name it. Their pockets were filled with these *pudiyas*. Different kinds of empty wrappers were also seen on the ground. In late fall, *pudiya* wrappers fluttered more than the dry leaves.

"Yes, I have heard that she does not go to other shops either. Her father had spoken to some shop owners. The consequences are, Gupta is closing his magazine shop and shifting to another market. We cannot see Afzal nowadays. He is grounded," another guy, Ghosh, added. He and his Bengali friends were using the ground for *pandaal* and Durga Puja.

"*Bhujang Bhaiya*, did you really find her kissing that guy from Meerut?" Deemak demanded with a mouth filled with gutkha.

If there is something in this world that travels faster than light, it is rumour and gossip.

"No, she was not kissing him, and that is just a rumour. She loves me. We were meeting at Bithoor, and that Sunil came and started misbehaving. So I smashed his face. Later Tunni's father got to know about it, and he sent her to Kota for better preparation of JEE," said Bhujang.

"Are you telling the truth? I have even heard that you did not fall from the stairs. It was Guddu Shukla who…" asked Deemak, looking at Bhujang's waistline, which was still wrapped with fresh bandages.

"*Humse kayde mein raha karo*. Don't cross your limit," Bhujang sneered. "What I say, is the truth. Now, let's focus on the plan. *Bechu Bhaiya* is leading this. Bengali, this time we will do *Bhashaan* through the DAV hostel area, and all of us will be Maa Durga's devotees in disguise. But instead of moving towards Moti Jheel, we will enter the hostel courtyard and then attack Guddu's people. First Sunil Chauhan, and then we will tackle Guddu Shukla."

Ghosh nodded. He was also shocked that Tunni had moved to Kota. Working for *Bechu Bhaiya* was a proud moment. Some of the Berra colony boys used to make fun of Ghosh that he was a coward. A yellow-belly. He had to prove that Benaglis were as courageous as *Kanpuriyas*. After all, revolutionaries like Khudi Ram Bose or Subhash Chandra Bose were Bengalis. He wanted to prove his point.

"Don't worry, the work will be done as per plan. Today, 2nd October is Mahashtami. Let's do it on Oct 5th, a day after Vijaydashmi," said Ghosh. "We will win, and we will kill this Ravan," he gave a war cry.

A look of satisfaction passed over Bhujang's face. He had convinced his colony guys that they were fighting for Bechu because Guddu Shukla had dared to come to this colony and misbehaved with their own colony girl, Rimjhim. Bhujang had managed to save his own pride and a false sense of dignity.

✳

A twenty-foot-high *protima*, (idol) of *Maa Durga* was pulled onto a truck. On another truck the statues of Ganesha, Laxmi, Kartika and Saraswati were kept. Bechu, Bhujang – who was still limping – Deemak, Ghosh and around thirty other boys from Barra applied red coloured *abeer*.

This irked Ghosh a little. *Bhashaan* in Kanpur was not as grand as Kolkata's. There was no '*Sindoor Khela*' among women and Pandals were not heavily decorated. The boys were throwing *abeer* more like *Ganesh Chaturthi* scenes of Bollywood movies. Here in Kanpur, Durga Puja looked so different.

Bechu rummaged in his backpack. He took out his pistol, checked whether it was loaded or not, and placed it back. Deemak and Ghosh looked at him, awestruck.

"You are making the same mistake again. I joined you because you insisted, but I don't approve of this nonsense," said Rishabh.

Bhujang gave a snide smile to Deemak and Ghosh.

"Rishabh, just the last time I'm asking for help. After that, I will immerse myself in the books," said Bechu.

"Show some guts. You Delhi-walas are chickenhearted, aren't you?" said Bhujang.

Rishabh ignored him, giving no reply. Sometimes it's better to follow the herd to avoid public shaming. Fools bring you to their own level and beat you, and you don't need to win each and every argument.

Afzal arrived on time with fifteen boys of Chamanganj. For Rishabh, many of them looked dangerous. They were in Pathan suits of various colours, some grey, some black and some green. They were carrying swords.

Ghosh and Bhujang approached them to apply *gulaal or abeer*, but they demurred. Bhujang reached Afzal. "You guys need to blend in. In this attire, you look totally different, and we will easily be caught. And remove your topi," snarled Bhujang insisting they comply.

"No. We cannot apply that *abeer* on our forehead," Afzal shrugged.

Bhujang looked towards Bechu for help. Bechu looked clueless, and he was also unaware of how to handle this situation now. Bhujang was right; they were looking extremely odd.

"You guys will get only five minutes, and after that, you will be smashing their skulls and vandalising the campus. Why don't you thirty-five people enter first, and then these fifteen can barge in on their bikes? Then they don't have to apply *abeer*, just tie a chunni on their head. Further, you guys don't need to use the swords. Use these hockey sticks. We are not going to kill anyone," suggested Rishabh.

"See, this is why I always ask him to join," Bechu turned towards Bhujang and sneered.

"Hide these sticks in the truck," commanded Bechu. He ignored all.

Everyone, other than Afzal's team, smeared the next round of *abeer* and wore chunnis. Then they screamed, "Mata rani ki jai, Durga mai ki jai."

The caravan moved ahead from Barra Maidaan to Civil Lines instead of Moti Jheel. Afzal checked his watch. He had to give a lead start to Bechu of five minutes.

Around thirty boys reached DAV boys hostel gate at Civil Lines. They were all dancing to tunes but alert. Two guys were beating dhol. An electric pole in the corner of the entry reminded Bechu about their first brawl with Sunil, the place where Sunil had tripped and fallen flat on his face.

Bechu jumped out of the truck and moved towards the gate while dancing. The gate was closed, and one old guard was at the gate.

"Bhujang, you be here, near the statue, as you have not fully recovered," said Bechu, and he looked at Afzal and Deemak. "You guys follow me. Others, take out your rackets, wickets, bats or hockey sticks, whatever weapon you are carrying."

Bechu tucked his pistol and marched towards the gate. Rishabh gave him a final severe look, making it rather clear that he felt he was making a grave mistake.

Bechu, Afzal and Deemak reached a rickety iron gate. They noticed Vinod Yadav and Rajiv Mahto were already present there. They whispered something in the guard's ear. The guard gave a look to Bechu, patted khaini on his palm and placed it in his mouth as if it was a big secret. Then, he disappeared in seconds.

"Our boys are on the fourth floor, there should be no harm done to them. Guddu is in his room, 21, and Sunil in 17. On the left side, you can find their bike and Jeep. They're parked. Ramshackle those first," said Vinod.

"We don't need you," said Bechu.

"I'm not doing it for you. I'm helping another Yadav," Vinod sneered. He glanced at Bhujang, who was sitting on the truck, holding his back.

"Don't do your Yadav politics here."

"Then what kind of politics should I do?"

"I don't know. I'm here for something else."

"Don't you think politics is everywhere? You are here for something, and that something is your politics. You are in Uttar Pradesh, and it's the land of *Yaduvansis*. You cannot get away from it. Somewhere, sometimes, you have to face Yadav politics." Vinod folded his hand like a politician. He grinned at Bechu with mock-politeness and scurried away.

Bechu beckoned the truck driver, and the truck with the Durga idol entered the campus. The hostel students gathered, and they bowed to offer their respect. As per the plan, Bechu started distributing *prasaad*, but his eyes were scanning the hostel campus for his targets.

✳

It was eleven in the morning when the sun rays warmed Sunil's room. Waking up late in October was always a cosy one. Sunil rose from his fourposter and wrapped up the mosquito net. He heard the dhol beats and *mata ki jaykara*.

Sunil came out, and a five-foot-seven guy approached him, offering prasad. His face was smeared in *abeer*. Suddenly, Sunil heard a glass cracking and the sound of a bike revving. He looked to his right and saw a guy smash his Bajaj Pulsar bike and set fire on it. He now saw around fifteen Muslim boys on bikes enter the campus.

Sunil squinted his eyes at the guy who was standing in front of him. It was Bechu. The moment Sunil had identified him, Bechu slapped Sunil. It was a tight *kantaap*, and Sunil's ears heard a whistling silence for a few seconds.

"*Madharchod*," Sunil pushed Bechu. He ran, and he screamed, "*Maaro Chutiyon ko*, they have attacked our hostel."

Uma popped out from a first-floor room with an IIT-JEE mathematics prep guide in his hand. When he saw Bechu, he sprinted towards the boundary, jumped the wall, and ran away.

Bechu's men drew their hockey sticks from the truck and started smashing the campus. The first line of beating got the *bhakts* who came first for Durga offerings. There was chaos in the hostel, and students ran everywhere to save their lives.

"Hit everyone who does not have *abeer* on his face or is not wearing Pathan suit," screamed Bhujang. The sense of power gave him strength, and he also joined the party. He enjoyed the soothing sight where he could see that more than forty students of the DAV hostel were getting beatings. He picked the hockey stick up with a winning smile. It gave him courage, and he ran towards Sunil with his limping legs.

Sunil ran as if a tiger was roaring behind him to take his life. He tried to climb the stairs but fell from the second step. He felt as if he had seen this scene multiple times in his dreams, where he tried to run but could not. He fumbled and kept stumbling on the same step. His muscles gave up, and a deep sense of fear choked his voice. He saw Lala, who was at the railing of the second floor and trying to figure out from where the noise was coming.

"Lala, inform *Guddu Bhaiya* that our hostel is under attack. Bechu Mishra is here," Sunil screamed when Bechu came near him smoking a cigarette.

Bechu took the cigarette, inhaled a deep puff, and looked at the spark when it lit brightly in front.

"You guys enjoy frying butt, right?"

"Sorry, *Bechu Bhaiya.*"

"Don't you think this one is getting old? You were sorry a few months ago as well."

"This time, I'm sorry with all of my heart."

"Good. But why don't you be sorry by your *gand*?" Bechu examined his cigarette, took a pause, and shoved it in Sunil's ass.

Sunil screamed and writhed on the stairs. He saw that Lala was standing stunned, and his eyes were wide open.

"*Arey chutiye, bula na Guddu Bhiya ko.* Inform *Guddu Bhaiya*," cried Sunil. He looked at Lala with imploring eyes.

✳

Guddu heard the cacophony but ignored it. He skimmed through the *Hindu Newspaper* and read the editorial on Vajpayee and the importance of India-US ties. He marked some valuable and challenging political words like embargo, bipartisan, hustings, and looked for them in the dictionary.

Guddu's concentration broke when someone banged on his door.

"*Guddu Bhaiya, Guddu Bhaiya*, open the door," Lala barked while knocking on the door like a furious man.

"Wait. What happened? *Tumri amma kisi ke saath bhag gayi kya?* Did she elope with someone?" Guddu opened the door and showed his disappointment. "Go make a cup of tea for me."

"*Bhaiya*, my mother is dead, so she cannot elope with anyone. Can you come to the corridor and look down at the courtyard?"

Guddu saw the chaos. Students were running around and getting beatings from outsiders. He glanced at the stairway. A boy smeared in red *gulaal* was belting Sunil.

"*Ruko*. Stop this," Guddu roared.

Guddu's voice was so loud that around eighty guys came out from their room from the first and second floors. All were looking down at Guddu Shukla. Guddu looked down. From a few rooms across, he saw Vinod Yadav, and he was rubbing his *khaini*. His sidekick, Rajiv Mahto, flicked a pan-masala packet. He mocked Guddu's style, the same way Guddu had flicked in his room a few months ago when they were ragging Lala.

Guddu looked left, and he saw familiar faces: Dubey, Ajit, Suraj, Manjit, all were sheepishly staring at Guddu.

"Are you guys not ashamed? Your own brothers are fighting with locals, and you are getting entertained from your respective rooms?"

"*Bhaiya*, Vinod Yadav had said that we are not to get involved in this fight," Ajit said reluctantly. He had rubbed oil on his bald head.

"Now, you will listen to this loser! You decide what you guys want to do." Guddu's eyes pierced everyone. They all lowered their gaze, and they felt ashamed. Guddu was correct.

"This college has witnessed the greatness of Atal Bihari Vajpayee and I.K. Gujral, and they were students of our college. These few loafers cannot ruin its glory. I am going to my room to solve the analytical skill practice set. By the time I come out, this mess should be cleared up," said Guddu and walked inside his room.

Lala followed. Guddu pulled up his chair and sat on it. Calmly, Guddu grabbed a glass of water and took some sips, and adjusted the time on his alarm clock. He looked back. "Lala, could you please prepare a cup of tea. Make sure you add ginger," Guddu asked politely. He paused. "Prepare two cups, one for Bechu. We should welcome our guest." Then Guddu flipped some papers and started scribbling.

Hostel boys ran to their room and picked hockey sticks, bottles, swords whatever suitable weapons they found. Vinod Yadav tried to convince them and opposed the direction which Guddu had given, but it was in vain.

"*Guddu Bhaiya* is right. Vajpayee Ji's and I.K. Gujral's respect is at stake. Let us teach these guys a lesson," bellowed Ajit, rubbing his shiny bald head, which smelled of mustard oil. The other students roared, and they ran down.

It was like revolutionaries storming the barricades. The new stream of students with full vigour and energy attacked Bechu's boys. They started smashing and thrashing people who were in red scarves or *Pathan* suits. Now for every Barra colony boy, there were two DAV hostel posses.

Finding the right moment, Sunil pushed Bechu and ran away to his room, locking it behind him. He had no energy to fight back or take revenge, and he dropped onto his bed.

Bechu tried to help his friends, smashing some glass bottles on opponents' heads or driving hockey sticks into others' backs. He noticed that even Rishabh was fighting, and he threw some punches at hostel residents. But eventually, Rishabh got caught and endured a few hockey sticks to his shoulders.

After ten minutes, Bechu noticed that he was losing the turf. Half of his men were on the ground writhing or getting beatings. Nervously, he rummaged at his waistline.

There was the sound of a gunshot. All stood in their places, and no one moved. The eyes were on Bechu, and he had fired the pistol in the air.

In the room, Guddu heard the gunfire. He cringed and shrugged off Lala when he brought the teacup. Guddu drew his iron trunk, which was kept beneath the bed. He opened it. It was full of different kinds of weapons: pistols, double-barrel rifles, revolvers. He picked pistols randomly. They were shiny, heavy and foreign-made. After examining them for a few seconds, he tucked them in his trousers.

He walked out of his room and took the stairs to come down. The hostel boys heard the familiar footsteps, and everyone's eyes followed Guddu Shukla. Guddu's arrogance was at a peak. He noticed a guy holding a gun in the crowd and walking towards him.

Reading people's body language and their horrified faces, for Guddu, it was easy to recognise the leader of the crowd. He scanned Bechu from head to toe.

Bechu looked up slightly. Guddu's towering height and persona did not intimidate him. Guddu picked a Mauser from his trousers, checked if it was loaded and threw it at Bechu.

"*Mishra Ji Ram Ram*. From the bottom of my heart, I wanted to meet you," said Guddu.

Hearing the gunshot, Sunil had also come out from his room. He chuckled when he saw the way Guddu introduced himself. Guddu looked at Sunil and threw another pistol to him, which Sunil caught like a professional cricketer.

"You might not be aware of me. We have never met. I'm Guddu Shukla, or you can say, Himanshu Shukla."

Bechu's gang members gathered behind Bechu. Guddu noticed a guy in the red shirt, and it was Bhujang. Others were radiating anxiety. For Guddu, it was easy to read, and this was food for him, others' fear.

The pistol was still lying on the floor.

"See that carefully. What you are holding is a *desi katta*, a locally made pistol. It can explode after two shots, and you have already made one. The next one, it might go off in your hand. *Tab tumhari gand fategi*," Guddu sighed, took a pause and then continued. "I know you are not here for this *chutiya* Bhujang, and also, I did not help Sunil although I consider him a younger brother. We all are here for one cause, for one girl... Rimjhim. But, Rimjhim cannot be yours. She is mine, and eventually, I will marry her. Now she lives in your house as a tenant, so *baraat* will come to your place. *Maa kasam*, I will enjoy the *naagin* dance in front of your house."

"Guddu, stop your nonsense," Bechu gripped the gun tightly.

"*Misir Ji*, you cannot do anything apart from swelling your nostril, and it's already bulging with anger. I'm repeating, you cannot do anything. *Hum maar lengey tumhari aur likh dengey Kranti.* Do you understand the meaning of this local adage?"

"*Kranti likhna sab samjhte hain bhaiya,* everyone knows. *Guddu Bhaiya,* will you write with pen or charcoal?" sneered Sunil.

Infuriated and insulted, Bechu raised his gun and aimed it at Guddu. Bechu was shaking and trembling with anger. Everyone was startled.

"Bechu, hold your gun down," Rishabh screamed.

Bechu's action irked Guddu. He had confidence that Bechu could not fire a gun at someone. A guy who was serious about his studies and career would never do something like that.

"This is what I call *Indiyapa*. I think I have to write *Kranti* on your sister and mother's...."

A second gunshot rang out, and everyone's ears filled with a constant static sound.

Guddu thought that he had temporarily gone deaf. The static hissed for a few seconds in his ear, then Guddu realised that he might have been shot. He looked at his body and looked down, and a stream of blood spluttered.

Shocked Guddu did not feel any pain, he looked to his right.

Sunil was standing and looking at him, petrified. Confirming that he did not get the bullet, he looked back at Guddu.

Guddu moved right when a lean body crashed on his shoulder with a rattling sound of a teacup. It was Lala.

Guddu held Lala in his arms. "*Abey*, someone call an ambulance. Does anyone have a mobile phone?" Guddu screamed.

At the same time, a police siren blared. Like in movies, this was the Indian police, always at the right moment, but at the wrong time.

Students scurried away. Ghosh and his friend ran and jumped the wall to escape. They left their truck behind. Other hostel students grabbed whatever they could, closed their rooms hastily, and ran towards the back gate.

"See you behind Tunni's house," said Afzal to Rishabh. Afzal pulled Bhujang and forcibly pushed him to sit on his bike. Other Muslim guys started their bikes and wheeled through the front gate.

No one offered Bechu any help. Rishabh grabbed Bechu's hand and ran towards the rickety back gate with all the other students. Bechu's hand was cold and drenched with sweat.

Rishabh followed the same path as other students and came out of the hostel through the back gate.

By the time the police parked their Jeep and got active, many of the students and hooligans had vanished from the scene. Police found only Sunil and Guddu, sullied in blood and holding the body of Lala.

"Ambulance," he screamed, looking into the familiar face of the police inspector.

When Bechu and Rishabh reached Azad Maidan, behind Tunni's house near Barra Bazar, they found Bhujang and Afzal waiting. Afzal had turned purple with fear. His shirt was drenched with sweat. Bhujang was holding his waist, and shooting of pain was visible on his brows.

"I'm going to my town, Saharanpur," Afzal declared. "*Bhujang Bhaiya*, take care of my bike. I will come back and collect it after a few months."

"You guys left us and ran away," said Rishabh.

"I had only one place. I chose Bhujang because he was injured, and he could not run," replied Afzal.

"It's okay. I'm capable of taking care of myself," said Bechu.

Without saying goodbye, with a trembling heart, Afzal turned around and strolled to leave. But he thought for a moment and turned back. "*Bechu Bhaiya*, can I say something?"

"What?"

"I did not murder that guy." Afzal looked at the ground, ignoring eye contact.

"We all know. Why did you say that?"

"No, you guys are all from prominent families. Your parents will do everything to save you. I'm a small vendor. I sell *chaat-samosa*, and I earn merely a hundred rupees a day," said Afzal.

"So how does it matter, Afzal. We have all known you for a long time. You and Bhujang are equal for me," said Bechu.

Bhujang looked at Bechu. He did not like this comparison. How could a *chat-wala* be equal to him? Bhujang was better. He felt terrible and looked at Bechu helplessly. First, Rishabh came a few years ago and replaced him, now Bechu was saying Afzal was his equal.

"No, *Bechu Bhaiya*. We are not equal. You know, a long time back, Gupta had said something very wise. Only in movies can a *taxi-wala* or people like us dream of a beautiful girl. You cannot find a Raja Hindustani in real life. My only mistake was that I liked Tunni. For her, for my love, I got involved. Now, the police will open an interrogation. They will make enquiries as to who was there at the crime scene. Instead of you, they will try to find a scapegoat based on some of your family's influence and pressure. I'm the perfect fit." Afzal's voice choked, and tears escaped from his eyes. "I'm the perfect fit to declare the murderer. A poor Muslim always suffers. I have heard it. I have seen this in movies also."

"This will not happen, Afzal," Bechu grabbed Afzal's hand and hugged him. "I committed the crime, and I will go to jail. I won't let it happen, don't even think like that."

"*Bhaiya*, I promise you I will become a good man. My father had a woodwork business in Saharanpur. Due to the lousy economy and scarcity of wood, it suffered, so I came down south of UP to earn money. I have some land. Now I know this food business. I will sell that land and, with that money, start a catering business. Will take contracts for marriages and events. When you get married to Rimjhim, I will serve the food for free. I promise you."

"Afzal, go to your native place and don't worry. I will get out of this mess, and I promise you, you will not be a scapegoat."

Afzal wiped his tears, gave everyone a hopeful gaze, and bade them all a goodbye, "*Khuda Haafiz.*"

✳

"I said before, don't even try to use the gun," bellowed Rishabh when he noticed that Afzal was out of their earshot.

"It was a mistake, happened in the heat of the moment," said Bhujang.

"Bhujang, you square head, just shut up!" Rishabh screamed.

"What will happen?" Bechu's worry emerged for the first time. He wiped his head with a shaking hand.

"As Afzal was saying, there will be a police case, and we all will be behind bars. It's a non-bailable offence. Forget about your CA dreams," said Rishabh.

"CA, CA, CA," repeated Bhujang frantically. "How selfish you are. Every time you talk about your stupid life goal and dreams. Bechu and I were happy with our small life goals, then you came, and you snatched every ounce of happiness from our lives. Screw CA," Bhujang yelled.

"Bhujang," Rishabh raised his finger in a threatening manner, "it's all happened because of you. That Kanpur dame, Tunni, she doesn't even give a damn about you. *Tere ko ghass tak nahi daalti.* She roams with Sunil. And you, like a red-bottomed baboon, trying to get attention like a clown. And this shithead, he is firing a gun and killing people for you," Rishabh fumed with anger.

Bhujang's eyes welled up. A simple truth shattered his heart again, and this was more painful than the day he had seen Sunil and Tunni snogging each other.

"*Sale Chiraand kism ke insaan ho be*. You won't understand love. *Teri wali to gayi uper*. The one who loved you committed suicide," Bhujang blurted. Then he realized that he had made a blunder, and he immediately looked at Bechu.

Bechu, who was till now not focusing on the conversation, picked up the word suicide. The word he hated so much. His hand acted in the blink of a second, and he slapped Rishabh. Rishabh fell on the ground, and his lip cut.

"*Sala madharchod*, it was you," said Bechu, his voice shaking, his eyes bright red. "It was you. Because of you, Shruti, my baby sister, committed suicide." Bechu felt betrayed, and it was the biggest sin in the world: his best friend had been involved with his sister.

Rishabh tried to get to his feet. He gave a disgusted look to Bhujang, who had revealed a long-hidden secret. Bhujang lowered his gaze.

Bechu picked up his pistol and put it to Rishabh's forehead.

"Will you hear me first, or are going to kill me without knowing my side of the story?" Rishabh looked into Bechu's eyes.

The wind did not blow, not a single tree swayed. The ominous silence overtook Rishabh's heart before he turned to rummage in his archived memories of Shruti.

Guddu adjusted his feet on the table. The wooden and plastic weaved chair in the police station was not comfortable.

"Do you want tea, *Guddu Bhaiya*?" asked the inspector who was sitting across from him. He noticed Guddu's leg on the table, a disrespectful way to behave with a senior inspector, but he said nothing.

"*Mangaao*, I would like to have. Can you switch on the fan?" ordered Guddu.

Guddu looked right, and he saw Sunil, Ajit, and a few more guys. More than ten were in the lockup.

A constable brought two cups of tea for Guddu and the inspector.

"Guddu Bhaiaya, have tea. *Chai pijiye*. Don't worry. *Yeh sab labhed hota rahta hai*," said Inspector Nikesh. He removed his cap and adjusted his hair, which was receding. "We are meeting after a long time. The last time we met in Kanpur Dehat was when you were capturing the booth. *Aapka bhaukal abhi bhi tight hai*." Nikesh grinned and took a sip.

"Switch on the fan," Inspector Nikesh asked the constable. "Why do you get into these brawls? *Ab ye bakaiti main kahe padtey hain?*"

"What could I do? *Ab ho gaya*," Guddu ignored the inspector.

There was a commotion in the police station. Most of the staff and officers were in uniform and made sure their desk or station was spotless. A few constables came and gestured to the inspector, that he should be ready now. Nikesh jumped up from his seat and sprinted towards the gate. Guddu disregarded these movements and sipped his tea.

A white ambassador car whose headlight was covered came and stopped at the gate. The driver in white uniform immediately came out from his seat and opened the car door. A man in a grey safari suit jostled with a file in hand. Nikesh noticed *parivahan mantralay*, ministry of transportation, on the number plate.

R.C. Shukla came down, and he entered the police station in a white dhoti and starched kurta. He was fifty-five but active. He stroked his shoe-brush moustache and looked around.

"Sir, *Guddu Bhaiya* is sitting in my chamber. I have not filed the case yet," Nikesh reported like an obedient child. "Sir, sit here," Inspector Nikesh drew his chair and offered to the minister.

"I hope this has not reached the media – you have managed it," R.C. Shukla said to his assistant who was standing in safari.

R.C. Shukla looked at Guddu. Guddu sipped his tea and arrogantly put the empty cup down on the table so loudly it forced R.C. Shukla to glare at Guddu angrily. The police station staff, constables, and inspector all got startled.

"I am not here to sit. I'm here because this guy got himself into trouble," said the minister. He grew agitated when

Guddu ignored him. The sound of a pedestal fan whirling echoed throughout the room. A constable came running with another teacup, for the minister.

"What game are you playing with me? What do you want to do in life?" asked R.C. Shukla.

"Nothing." Guddu picked up a biscuit, analysed the packet. He dipped the biscuit in the cup that had been brought for R.C. Shukla. When he removed the biscuit, half fell back into the teacup.

"What kind of *gundagardi* and rowdyism are you spreading inside the university hostel?" asked R.C. Shukla.

"I told you, I have quit politics, and I'm studying there. I'm preparing for an MBA entrance exam."

"Entrance exams?" R.C. Shukla rummaged in his pocket, removing his blue Nokia mobile phone wrapped in thick plastic. "Which college do you need admission to? You tell me, I will get you in." He handed his phone to his assistant and said, "Call the education minister."

"I don't need your charity. I'm capable of passing the exam," Guddu said in frustration.

"Guddu, look at the sons of other ministers. They help their fathers. Join the party again, be a politician. It's in your DNA. I will arrange a party ticket for you in the next election. Kalpi or Unnao will be a good seat for you."

"Other politicians' sons? If I need to be like them, I have to shoot a model who refused to serve me alcohol. If I need to be like your other politicians' son, I must drive a BMW into the people who sleep on the street. Tell me, should I be like them?" Guddu stood and leaned on the table. "*Hum jaisey bhi hain*, I'm better than those *chiraands*."

R.C. Shukla felt that the portraits of Gandhi and Subash, which were hanging on the police station wall, were staring at him. He looked around the police station. The police officers and people in the lockup were stunned, probably because they had been unaware that Guddu Shukla was his son until now. Inspector Nikesh wore a look of pride because he was close to the minister and was informed of this.

"It's okay, do whatever you want," said R.C. Shukla hastily.

"If I was acting like a politician's kid, I would not have been here for a small brawl. Maybe I would have been here for a rape case," murmured Guddu. He was on his chair and again, calmly picking up biscuits.

"So you are still angry with me and trying to punish me," asked R.C. Shukla.

"Punish you for what?"

"For the death of your mother. It was not my mistake."

"A politician does not make a mistake, and it's always a commoner's fault for trusting them. I never blamed you for that accident, and it's your guilt that always asks for my forgiveness." Guddu looked into his father's eyes. "Isn't it?"

"Guddu, that road was built by a corrupt contractor. Yes, I was a transport minister then, but...."

"*Neta Ji,* I believed you for ten years. My mother's car had an accident because of a big pothole, and she could not reach the hospital on time because of the same road, which was a scam. That contractor was a scapegoat, and the tender was given to him only for the namesake. A few years back, I saw those papers and decided to leave the party. I know you were the trustee of that company. That's it. I'm not joining you in politics again. What an irony: after ten years, you are again a transport minister. I hope, in this tenure, no one will die because of the conditions of the road."

R.C. Shukla clenched the corner of his dhoti. He looked down, rummaged in his kurta's pocket, pulled out his glasses, and put them on. It was his technique to look confident and composed to think what his following action should be.

"The guy who fired the gun… put him behind bars, but make sure Guddu's name is not mentioned," R.C. Shukla said to the inspector. Like a politician, he ignored Guddu's last words. He handed two packets to the inspector. "One for you, and one to distribute to other staff. I have already sent some gifts to your seniors."

Nikesh quickly grabbed the packets and placed them inside the table drawer, without counting them.

"It's not needed. It was my mistake, as I crossed the line. I abused and swore at his mother and sister. He lost his temper and fired the gun. If I were there in his place, I would have done the same thing. And, my aim is perfect, and it would have hit the target." Guddu gulped the tea down in one shot. "Nikesh, sir, there is no sugar in the tea. Can you order one more?"

Inspector Nikesh turned towards minister Shukla and gave his assurance. "Don't worry, minister sir, I will manage the case, and it won't get into the media. You go home and relax."

R.C. Shukla looked at his son. He wanted to hug him before leaving, but he did not. Instead, he placed a new mobile phone on the table.

"It's for you. Call me when you are in need," said R.C. Shukla.

He turned around and walked towards the door. Other police staff moved, and they all ran towards the white ambassador car.

Nikesh opened the car door for R.C. Shukla and whispered in his ear, "I will try to put a word in his ear."

✳

A constable came and served tea for the people in the lockup. Ghosh was sitting in the corner, he was the only guy from Bechu's side who got caught, and he jumped up first and grabbed the teacup.

"*Guddu Bhaiya*, I'm innocent. I came here only for *visharjan*," Ghosh shouted to make sure he was heard. He deliberately put on his original Bengali accent to show he was an outsider. He was not a *Kanpuriya*. "They forced me to do this."

"I know. You guys keep quiet."

Inspector Nikesh came back after giving a farewell to the minister. He sat on his chair and looked at Guddu, and he was ready to impart the wisdom locked inside his receding grey-haired head.

"I know why you dislike your father. Why do you hate politics? You must be thinking that your mother was the victim of corruption. So you hate this system. But do you think you are also part of it? Your chosen world also has its problems, and you pick the facts according to your convenience. You cannot accept your father because you think he is corrupt. But you are okay sitting here on the chair instead of lockup. Conveniently, you choose your own corruption, but hate that of others," said Nikesh.

Guddu sat on the chair for a few minutes in uncomfortable silence. He rubbed the sweat of his hand on the coarse wooden arm of the chair, then he looked left towards his friends, who were in the lockup. A constable came and opened the lockup, the steel lock clanged when it was removed from the iron bars.

"We are releasing them. It's also your duty to see that these boys go home," said Nikesh while reading Guddu's expression. "Your father may be corrupt, but he is a nice man. He had a meeting with the chief minister and a few prominent political figures, and it was important for him to move forward to central politics. He could have made a phone call and gotten the work done. But for you, he came down here from Lucknow. Why? Because he cares for you."

"Thanks for the advice. I know there must be some extra packet you might have received. *Police wale free main kuch nahi kartey*," Guddu smirked.

Inspector Nikesh opened a file. He was happy to read files rather than breaking his head with a twenty-something brat who was the son of a powerful minister.

The guys surrounded Guddu to know the next steps. Guddu looked at Ghosh. "You go and perform your *visharjan*." Then he scanned the crowd. "Where is this Uma Pandey? Someone contact him and ask him to meet me. I have work for him," Guddu said and walked out of the police station, followed by his posse.

"*Durga mai ki, jai!*" Bengalis screamed and submerged the idol carefully in the Motijhil. Bhujang was sitting in silence. His eyes searched for Ghosh in the hope that he may get his glimpse, and Ghosh might have escaped and had some news about the guy who was shot.

Every idol looked the same, like the one from the colony. He noticed a board on which it was written, "Littering and dumping any object in the lake is prohibited." But *maa Durga* is not an object. Gods and goddesses have created everything, and they had the right to be immersed.

The greenish lake water became brown with a hue of red. Many idols were submerged. Bechu, Bhujang and Rishabh were sitting at an iron bar, which had probably been set there for barbells for an open park gym. Even in this heavenly and spiritual discord, there was silence among them.

"I was immature. Three years ago, our friendship was new, and you were my only friend. I didn't know how it happened and when it happened," Rishabh broke the silence.

Then he saw few police constables, and fear crept in. Bechu felt uncomfortable. But the police passed them by. They were probably there to control the *visharjan*.

"I was new to the city, and seemingly your home was a second home for me. Aunty used to bestow her love on me like a son. Then I started talking with Shruti, and she used to ask me about music, guitar, and English songs. Later I noticed that she had developed an interest in my tastes. She used to ask me about Delhi. My early schooling in DPS. I opened up and started sharing my emotions more than needed. She liked me because I was different – different from Kanpur boys.

"Initially, I thought it was a normal affection. The kind of affection the younger sister of one's best friend shows. Once, she told me that she had a friend in the colony, Tunni, and she wanted to introduce me. That was the first warning sign. But I ignored it and went out with her to the mall to meet Tunni. I came to know that she was also from the same colony. I asked her if we couldn't have met in Barra itself, instead. But she showed me two movies ticket. I insisted that Tunni should also join, but Tunni winked at Shruti and left. Reluctantly, I watched the movie with Shruti.

"Then whenever I used to come to your house, I noticed that she used to hang around us. Sometimes brushing her hand with mine, sometimes trying to dishevel my hair or hold my hand. I was uncomfortable. I was scared. I liked her, but I was aware of the friendship code. Never encourage friends' sisters. I wanted to tell you, but I was overawed by you. I never dared to say anything to you. So, I limited my visits.

"One day, I came, and Shruti handed me a letter. I took it with a shaking hand and placed it in my pocket. Coming back home, I opened it with a pounding heart. The letter was in red text. Initially, I thought it was written in red ink. But it was blood. It was a love letter like you see in the movies.

"I was so scared that I did not go to your house for a week. But one day, you came and forced me to go home with you after our CA intermediate coaching classes. Shruti opened the door, and she got thrilled after seeing me. When she got a chance, she asked me what was my response to her letter. The next day her tenth-grade results were coming out. I asked her to focus on her studies. But she grabbed my hand and said she would die if I did not love her back. I did not know what to do, and I threatened that I would tell you. She was just fifteen, a schoolgirl. I left her in tears and went home.

"The next day, I heard that she had committed suicide. She ate sulphas tablets. It was the worst day of my life. I was lost. I came to your house, and there were police. They did not find any suicide notes or letters. I think she showed love to me even after dying. Everyone speculated it was because of her bad performance in the board exam." Rishabh's voice was choked. He struggled to swallow, and he looked at the sky. The evening breeze in the dark cloudy sky pierced his heart.

"For a few weeks, even I thought there was a chance it was the exam. But one day, Tunni came by, knocking on my door. She looked furious. She abused me first and started crying. She showed me the letter that Shruti had posted to Tunni, her best friend. Shruti had mentioned her failure in love and wrote that it was the lowest ebb of her life. I could read the pain she was going through. I told her why I did not reciprocate. Tunni gave me that letter, which I floated in the Ganges.

"After that, Tunni stopped talking with Bhujang. Bhujang confronted her, and she gave the excuse about Shruti's suicide. That day Bhujang came to me and exploded. After that, he always scorned me." Rishabh heaved a sigh and looked at Bechu. He knew Bechu was inconsolable.

"Rishabh, you go from here. I don't want to see you. Never, ever show me your face again," Bechu said in a stifled voice, not even looking at Rishabh.

Rishabh got to his feet. He looked at his friend one last time. "Bechu, if I had reciprocated her love, you might have killed me. If I knew that she would kill herself, I would have preferred dying from your bullet," said Rishabh, and walked off into the loud sound of *shankhs*.

A few strands of lake mist were hanging above the water surface in the cloudy sky. The Durga idols were now fully immersed and the sun was about to embrace the horizon.

The twilight turned to dusk and every moment passed like a snail before turning into a velvety black night. It poured heavily. Bechu was broken and devasted. He got an umbrella from Bhujang's house and distant police petrol siren brought a shiver to his body. He was sure that while returning to his home, there would be a police Jeep. He had made up his mind and practised his story. He had to live up to his friends' expectations. He would tell the truth and save his friends' lives and would take all the blame.

He was not sure who the guy was whom he had shot. Bechu had a faint recollection of a short guy, probably about his own height. He was standing next to Guddu, holding a cup of tea, elated with each discourse. Next, Bechu remembered him covered in blood. So much blood that now he might have been dead. The thought that he had killed someone jolted his stomach.

With a long stride, Bechu marched towards his home. Heavy droplets of rain splattered on the tin sheds. After a long time, he did not care about the muddy splashes making his trousers wet. His own hometown colony, Barra's Shyama Nagar, never looked so strange and weird before.

When he reached home, he was a little surprised. There was no police Jeep, but a big white Bolero and a familiar bike. His eyes grew wide open when he unbolted the rickety iron gate of his courtyard. The unoiled hinges squeaked and he saw a tall guy standing at Rimjhim's house door in a suit. With him, there was an aged man and woman. Probably they were parents of the guy. Shatrughan Singh looked happy, and he was showing his softer demeanour, folding his hand and bowing his head at every sentence the tall guy's father was uttering. Then Bechu looked at Rimjhim. She was in flashy glittering Banarasi sari. Bechu understood the matter in a second. When his eyes met with Rimjhim's, Bechu looked away hurriedly and increased his speed. He leapt on the stairs.

With some queer feeling, Bechu knocked on the door. The moment his father opened the door, he slapped him powerfully through the face. Bechu did not know that the old man could be so quick.

"You shot a guy?" bellowed Joginder Mishra, grabbing Bechu's hand and pulling him inside. Joginder Mishra quickly latched the door.

With deep guilt, Bechu lowered his head. He struggled to look his father in the eye. Regret didn't begin to encompass what he was feeling. Then Bechu heard a familiar voice. It was from the owner of the RX100.

"Don't worry, uncle. The situation is under control," Uma Pandey said to Bechu's father in a consoling but patronizing tone. "*Guddu Bhaiya* acted on it, and now the case is in his hand. The inspector is also ready. The guy who got shot is in the ICU. Thankfully he is out of danger and getting shifted to a bigger hospital in Lucknow for better treatment. He has confirmed that he will not file any complaint," Uma sneered.

Uma noticed that there was an awkward silence. Bechu, who was ridden with guilt, now was staring at Uma. Bechu's blood boiled with rage.

"Take these *ladoos*. Now let's kill our animosity. *Guddu Bhaiya* has forgiven you. On this happy occasion, eat *Thaggu ke Ladoo,* and he has sent these sweets," Uma said slyly.

"Uma. Just get out of my house," Bechu warned.

"This is how you treat your guest? He and his friends have done you a favour. You should be indebted to their kindness. But instead, you behave like this," Bechu's father yelled.

"I was going. I just want to convey that *Guddu Bhaiya* has forgiven you," Uma smiled at Bechu.

"He is a thorough gentleman," said Bechu's mother.

Uma dramatically lowered himself to touch Joginder Mishra's feet, then he bowed to Bechu's mother. Today, he was in traditional dress, white *Payjama-Kurta,* and had applied a tika on his forehead. He gave the impression of a homely and cultured boy-next-door image to Bechu's parents.

"*Chachiji, pranaam.* Now I will go. *Aagya dijiye,*" said Uma.

"Keep coming to visit, *beta,*" Bechu's mother said, wiping her moist eyes with the corner of her sari.

"Yes, aunty. This is my house too, and I keep coming here to meet your tenants. I know them," said Uma deliberately and tried to get into Bechu's nerves.

"Yes, they are good people," said Joginder Mishra.

"Ya, they have two lovely daughters. *Bahut pyaari bacchiyan hain,*" said Uma.

This made Bechu angry, and he lost his temper again. He knew that today Uma was a wolf in sheep's skin.

"*Chachaji*, this one extra packet of *ladoo*, just send it downstairs to the Singh family. The younger daughter, Rakshita, likes it a lot. I could have delivered it myself, but I'm in a hurry," said Uma as he scurried away. He was making sure that he was taking more time to irritate Bechu and get under his skin. Uma had never enjoyed such a situation before.

Bechu did not look at his parents as he just walked into his room. He noticed that Chotu was looking at him from behind the curtains, frightened, but he also did not say anything.

Bechu sank into his study chair, holding his head. He saw the picture of his dysfunctional family and cried. A family where his sister died three years ago, but no one talked about it, and they all pretended that nothing had happened. On her birthdays, everything was normal, and it was as if Shruti had never existed.

He picked up the picture and looked at Shruti. He tried to touch her... Bechu's memories made her alive. She was three years younger than him. Bechu remembered the good times. The red dress he selected for her birthday when Shruti was ten. He had to flick few bucks from his father's wallet. The soap bubbles they bought from Shimla. Instant noodles, which Shruti used to cook at home, especially for Bechu. Sunday mornings, they used to wake up early to watch *Ducktails* and *The Jungle Book*.

Bechu shirked again. He did not know when he and his sister grew up and drifted apart. Bechu remembered that Shruti had given him a hint. Once, she had asked Bechu, "What if I fell in love with someone?" "*Ek kantaap lagaunga*, I will kill that guy," Bechu had replied in anger. Remembering that, Bechu felt deep regret. He was a novice, and he was a teenager.

Bechu came back to his senses when he heard a screaming noise.

"*Tumne bigada ke rakha hai sabko*. You have spoilt them," Bechu's father was screaming at his wife. Bechu looked at his watch. It was 10:00 pm at night, and it must be Father's time to drink. It was not Joginder, but an old monk who spoke; an Amrish Puri howled.

Then Bechu heard the sound of glass shattering, and the smell of Old Monk filled his room. A few shards of glass skidded into Bechu's room through the gap at the bottom of the door.

"It's not because of me, it's you. You never bonded with them. Neither Bechu, Chotu nor with Shruti," Bechu's mother yelled. Till now, for so many years, she had bottled up her anger. "You were never there to listen to their problems. I cannot handle everything. There are many times, kids need their father's confidence. But all the time, you come home in an angry mood, drink at night and go to sleep. You are hardly available to listen to them. You are hardly there to solve their problem. I'm sick of your complaints and silent treatments," bellowed Bechu's mother.

Bechu had never heard his mother shouting or losing her temper. She should have shown this side of personality earlier. She yelled hysterically at her husband for a few minutes, and Joginder Mishra did not speak. After a few minutes of yelling and sobbing, a strange silence crept in.

✳

It had been a week, but Rimjhim had not seen Bechu, and she wanted to meet and talk to him. She had often gone to the rooftop to collect the laundry after it had dried, but Bechu did not show up. A phone rang, and Rimjhim's heart dropped. She was aware that the family of the guy who had come to see her would make their decision soon.

Shatrughan Singh picked up the phone. He listened to the call and kept saying "Hmm" and nodding his head. It was a complicated situation for Rimjhim to decipher. Rakshita and her mother were excited.

Shatrughan hung up the phone and turned towards his wife. "They are asking for the marriage at the end of December," said Shatrughan.

"The end of December? But that time will be *Kharmas*. It's inauspicious," said Rimjhim's mother.

"The guy has to go back to America. He is going to Singapore for a minor assignment, will be here in December for a few weeks and then wants to fly to the US with Rimjhim. He liked her," said Shatrughan.

Dejected, Rimjhim went back to her room. This was the fate of most girls in a small town. No one asks them if they want to marry or not. In a patriarchal society, the male family leader's decisions are final and unquestioned.

Rakshita came back from her bath. She flipped her hair and tossed it using a towel, and then finally she wrapped it. She rummaged through the gifts that her sister's suitor's family had given them. She examined Dior perfume, a Louis Vuitton bag, and a makeup kit from Estee Lauder.

Rakshita picked up a lip-gloss and looked at Rimjhim. "Can I use some?" she asked.

"Sure," Rimjhim replied, disinterested.

Rakshita applied the lip-gloss and pouted in the mirror.

"What's the occasion?" asked Rimjhim when she noticed Rakshita's attempt to look good. Rimjhim placed cotton balls carefully between her toes and applied nail enamel.

"Do you know you are the beauty number one of Kanpur?"

"What? From where did you get this ranking, and why are you telling me this?"

"This rank is given by the DAV hostel guys. I'm number two. I'm applying this makeup, lip-gloss, eyeliner because I want to maintain my rank. Uma told me about this," grinned Rakshita.

"Do you have a date with Uma again?" asked Rimjhim

"No, not this week."

"Do you love him?"

"It does not matter. I'm just nineteen years old. I'm not thinking about love or marriage. I have time. But do you like this guy, Mr America? I liked him," said Rakshita.

"Then why don't you get married to him?" asked Rimjhim.

"Wait, why are you saying this? That guy is good. He is intelligent, educated, a software engineer, settled in the US. What else do you want?"

"I don't know. I am feeling weird. I feel like it's not my heart that is pumping the blood in my veins, but my stomach."

"So, you don't like a software engineer, but rather a chartered accountant?"

"I don't know, I don't even know what this chartered accountant wants. I think he likes me, but I'm not sure."

"Then go and ask him."

"How can I ask directly? Maybe he is just kind to me, and I'm overthinking it. If he says no, I will look stupid." Rimjhim scratched her head.

"I think he likes you. I have seen sparkles in his eyes when he sees you." Rakshita paused for a moment to ponder. "Do one thing. Why don't you go and talk about your marriage prospects? Try to read his expression. If he becomes sad, then you know he loves you. Then talk about your feelings."

"Even if he does love me, his father will not agree to the marriage. He is a brahmin, and we are *thakurs*."

"Then go for QSQT."

"QSQT?"

"*Qayamat se Qayamat tak*. Elope with Bechu. To save the family's *izzat and* honour, I will marry Mr America," said Rakshita dramatically.

"You really are theatrical," said Rimjhim, and threw a cotton ball at Rakshita.

"Not theatrical, I'm romantic. And yes, in any case, this room will be mine. Many guys in the market are attracted to me, and I need some privacy to talk to them."

"What, are you insane?" Rimjhim gasped again. She knew her sister was a babble.

"I'm young, *The Bold and the Beautiful* type. I enjoy variety. For me, in layman's terms, someone has good silky hair, and someone else's chest is broad. Some get dimples in their cheeks or chin, and someone has a heart-stopping smile... They are all different... I don't know how girls settle with one," Rakshita said with a wink.

❋

The doorbell rang. Bechu's mother opened it and saw Rimjhim standing in front of her. She was in a pink chiffon suit, and the colour had enhanced the features of her face. Rimjhim looked like a model in a *Fair & Lovely* advertisement, glazed with pink light. Mother noticed the brass pot in Rimjhim's hand and polythene bag hanging in another.

"What have you brought?" asked Sumati, pointing at the pot with a smile.

"I brought *gaajar halwaa*. Chotu likes it, so I thought to share it with him. I cooked it today."

"Oh yes, he is in Bechu's room. Careful, Bechu is studying. His exams are in two weeks, and he gets easily irritated if he is disturbed."

"I will give it to him. He may like it," said Rimjhim. She picked a maroon sweater from her bag. "I completed this, and you can give it to him. The exams are in winter. He can wear it for good luck."

"You did more work on it than me. Why don't you give it to him?" said Bechu's mother with a warm smile. In Rimjhim's eyes, she was the perfect mother-in-law.

With a racing heart, Rimjhim entered the room. The sound of Rimjhim's footsteps made Bechu turn. Their eyes met, and Rimjhim again forgot why she was here. Bechu's gaze always made her lose her sense of time and place, and tranquillity embraced her. She composed herself when she heard Bechu's voice.

"*Halwaa*. What is the occasion?" asked Bechu.

"Before that, here is your gift," Rimjhim handed him the sweater.

"Oh, thank you. So getting *Grihsobha* from Gupta's shop was finally fruitful."

"Yes, and good luck with your exam." Rimjhim looked at all the calendars and schedules Bechu had stuck on the wall across the table. "It must be difficult."

"Yes, the pass rate is eight per cent." Bechu took a spoon from Rimjhim's hand. Their fingers brushed, which created an electric sensation in Rimjhim's heart. She had never before felt the way she felt for Bechu. Maybe this was love, she thought. But she was unable to tell if Bechu felt the same way.

"I'm getting married. A few weeks ago, you saw a guy at the door. He is my fiancé," said Rimjhim. She lowered her gaze. She was hoping Bechu would be surprised or may say something that she wanted to hear.

"Congratulations," said Bechu with a wide smile.

Rimjhim looked at him. Bechu's face was expressionless.

"The guy wants to get married by the end of December – he has to go to America."

"Do you like him?" asked Bechu, looking at the pages of the CA Scanner book, a set of past question papers.

"The guy is handsome. He earns good money. What else do I need?" said Rimjhim, thinking that slight exaggeration may wrench Bechu's heart, and force him to give her some indication of his feelings. She thought, *Please tell me you love me. Please tell me you cannot live without me.*

"Well, then it's time to eat some more sweets."

Bechu picked up a spoon and scooped out *halwaa* from the bowl. This time his fingers did not brush Rimjhim's. Chotu came running to the room, and Bechu put the spoon in Chotu's mouth. Rimjhim tried hard to know what was going on in Bechu's mind.

"Don't forget us after going to America. Bhool mat jaana," said Bechu.

Confused, Rimjhim walked towards the door. "I will try," she said.

I will try to forget you, Rimjhim said to herself.

November is wintertime in Kanpur, and the Ganges plains become chilly in the morning. Bechu squinted outside the misty window and noticed the foggy breath of the hawkers.

Bechu pulled his maroon sweater on and gazed at it for a few seconds. His mother and Rimjhim had knitted it for him, and it was special. He pulled it on and lit a *diya* in front of Lord Ganesha. He looked at his watch: he had fifty minutes until the exam. He had already had many dreams where he arrived late to the examination and tried to run to get there on time but could not. The day before yesterday, his dream was the worst yet: his examination paper was in Sanskrit, and he could not understand a single word.

He hated the November exams. Half of the time, his brain became numb due to cold, and it was difficult to recall what he had studied. Bechu rolled a few rotis and stuffed them in his mouth, and sprinted towards the door. He had to go to *Vidya Mandir Mahila Mahavidyalaya* which was thirty minutes away.

"Eat a spoonful of curd," mother shouted.

Bechu came back, hastily jammed the spoon in his mouth, and ran towards the stairs.

Bechu felt that a glimpse of Rimjhim could also bring him some luck, but he dumped the idea in fractions of a second. He did not want to think about her – he needed to focus only on his three-hour-long paper.

Bechu took an auto, and he saw Uma Pandey patrolling in the area for Rakshita. In the next two weeks, he had to write eight papers, from Financial Reporting to Indirect Tax Laws. It was better that he focused on this, leaving the others to deal with later.

He skimmed through his notes on Indian Accounting Standards when he saw a *hijra* approaching him at a red traffic light at Barra Bazar. Bechu reached into his wallet and drew out a fifty-rupee note. On exam day, he did not want to take any risks. The *hijra* gave him blessings and asked him what wish he wanted to be fulfilled. Bechu was surprised. Instead of thinking about passing the CA final exam, he asked for Rimjhim.

Last year Bechu had flunked financial reporting, but this year's paper was comparatively easy. He was able to answer the valuation of liability, shares and tangible fixed assets problems. When he came out of the class, he saw Rishabh. He wanted to ask how his exam had gone, but the thought of betrayal, and Shruti, resurfaced in his memory. He ignored Rishabh. Bechu had to prepare for the next day, Strategic Financial Management.

The exam week passed, and he wrote his last paper, the one he hated most: Indirect Laws. He wrote a lengthy essay on Foreign Trade Policy and its salient features. Bechu was surprised to see Rishabh in these exams. Rishabh had previously mentioned that he would appear only in Group 1. Liar.

✳

"Why are you so tense?" asked Bhujang when he saw Bechu in a gloomy mood.

Bechu did not hear. He and Bhujang stared at the River Ganges at Patthar Ghat for a moment. The evening breeze was chilling. Bhujang gazed at the step where he had grabbed Tunni's hand and had abused Sunil. Now Tunni was far away from him, in Kota, preparing for JEE. He felt stupid.

Three familiar *pujaris* came and glared at Bhujang. Months ago, they had picked him up in an unconscious state and called the ambulance. The memory brought more chills to Bhujang, and the pujaris went ahead and started performing Ganga aarti.

Ganga aarti at Kanpur's Patthar ghat was not as grand as at Bhujang Yadav's ancestral town Varanasi, but it was still a treat. Many gleaming *diyas*, incense sticks, and the sound of the *shankh* reverberated the holiness in their soul.

"My exams are over, so I came here for blessings," said Bechu.

"How was it? Will you pass this time?"

"I hope so. It was better than last year."

"Then you should be happy. *Pass ho jana tho mithai bhej dena Lucknow.*"

"Lucknow?" asked Bechu.

"Yes, I'm going to Lucknow. Last night, I had a man-to-man conversation with my father. I told him that I could not study further. I don't get a single word related to studies. Inspired by Afzal, I asked him to sell our ancestral property of Varanasi and give me that money for a business. For the gym. After a lengthy discussion, he agreed. But he said I first have to prove to him that I can run it. So, I will try to get a job in Lucknow as a fitness trainer in a big gym. I have selected a few to apply to. I will learn the nuances and then open my dream gym here in Kanpur."

"It's good that you have clarity in life."

"Why? You don't?"

Bechu waited for a minute and pretended that he was listening to Ganga aarti, *Om jai Gangey mata.* A few tourists and locals joined the pujaris and started singing loudly. The thought that he would soon have to part with Bhujang weighed on his heart.

"Being a CA was never my dream. When I got admission to B.Com., I had no clue what I would do. What should be my career... I went to the CA institute because some seniors advised me. There, I met Rishabh. He was inspiring. Then his dream became my dream. Now I'm so close to achieving it, and he is not there with me."

"Yesterday, I went to his home to meet him," said Bhujang.

"You went to see Rishabh?"

"Yes, but I could not find him. His apartment was vacant. But I met his mother."

"You met his mother! I have never seen her in the past three years," Bechu was surprised.

"Yes. I was feeling guilty after revealing his secret. I know he was not responsible. I was blaming him because of this event – because Tunni, our school friend, stopped talking with me. I had feelings for her and she rejected all my advances. I was immature. I guess, years ago, she did not believe in love. Tunni and I grew apart. She is ambitious, and I haven't even passed the twelfth grade. I lie to people that I'm a B.A. History student. I understand she was never attracted to me. If you chase a girl, she slips away. I understood that a little late."

"What did she say? Where did Rishabh go?" asked Bechu. Bechu was least interested in Bhujang and Tunni's story.

"He is back at his father's house."

"Back at his father's house? But his father died long ago."

"Yes, that is true. Two years after his father's death, his mother married a Punjabi businessman from Delhi. Rishabh had a hard time accepting him as his father. Rishabh's mother was a working woman, and she got a transfer from her office to Kanpur. Rishabh moved here too. He liked this place, and he liked us... Despite that, I was so mean to him."

"He was mean towards you too," said Bechu. He did not know why, but he could not listen to a single positive word spoken about Rishabh.

"I used to think the same, but...."

"But what?"

"But now I think I got it wrong. His mother knew me, and she talked about how Rishabh always spoke highly of us. That I have a dream – a dream of opening a gym. I had never seen respect for myself in anyone's parents' eyes. All my friends' parents look at me as a failure. But his mother treated me as a winner. She gave me hope. She gave me the courage to win. Why? Because Rishabh must have planted that notion. I had the audacity to talk to my father because of her. Because of the validation, I saw in Rishabh's mother's eyes..." said Bhujang. His voice was choked.

"I believed in your abilities as well."

"Bechu, I'm not comparing. I used to compare. I was always jealous of Rishabh, of how he could replace me in your affections. How could he become one of your best friends within three years? I was wrong. I was insecure. He was the perfect fit. Best friends have the same dreams, the same passion. I should have been okay with it. I got his Delhi number for you. Do you want it?"

Bhujang extended his hand, holding a chit he tried to hand to Bechu.

Bechu threw it in the river. "Best friends don't betray one another. They don't get involved with each other's sisters," said Bechu calmly.

"He was not."

An uncomfortable silence fell between them again. Bhujang was aware of Bechu's silent treatment.

"I have heard the news," said Bhujang.

Bechu looked at Bhujang and frowned.

"Rimjhim is getting married." Bhujang put a hand on Bechu's shoulder. "I will arrange everything. You guys elope and come to Lucknow. In March, your results will come. You will become a CA, and financially you can manage."

✳

The coffee machine hissed and steamed, and Uma inhaled the whiff of dark roasted coffee beans. He always liked the scent of Rave 3 Mall at Tilak Nagar. The aroma of essential oils from hand-made soap shops and the new clothing from Tommy Hilfiger, which he could not afford, were always inviting. This was his third date at Rave 3 Mall. He examined his pocket and counted the money. The three five-hundred-rupee notes that he had flicked from his father's pocket would suffice for today. But Rakshita had mentioned that she had to do some shopping, and he was worried about those expenses.

Rakshita added extra mayonnaise to her KFC ginger chicken burger and munched it. Uma had only a small coffee, to be economical – he said he had eaten a late lunch, so he was full.

Rakshita and Umanath took the escalator and reached the top floor. Their movie, *Tere Naam*, was due to start in twenty minutes. It had been released months ago, and Uma was eager to watch the new film 'Kal Ho Naa Ho', but it was not released yet. *Tere Naam* was attracting fewer crowds. Rakshita never asked why they were watching an old film.

They glanced through some film posters and entered the hall. Uma had booked the corner seat, but there were hardly four people watching this in Gold Class. Seeing that it was less crowded, Rakshita winked. Uma took the middle row, and this time he held Rakshita's hand. Rakshita smiled.

After a few scenes, a song started. The actress desired to dance while hiding behind *dupatta* and *odhani*. She declared that her heart was a foreigner.

Rakshita kept her face on Uma's shoulder. Uma had read many articles in *Cosmopolitan* magazines, like "20 signs a girl wants to kiss you." Uma leaned right and brushed his lips to hers. Rakshita adjusted and grabbed Uma's shirt. She opened his shirt's buttons and kissed him passionately. Uma slid his hand inside her *kurti*. He gently touched her breast. Rakshita moaned. For the next five minutes, they did not care if Salman Khan's character, Radhe, was devastated in love.

For an hour, Rakshita tried a pink *lehenga* and asked the tailor to adjust the A-line and make the choli backless.

"You are looking like a bride. Are you attending any cousin's marriage?" asked Uma.

"No, Rimjhim is getting married."

"What? How come so soon?"

"It doesn't matter to you, and it got fixed a few months back."

"Are you not going to invite me?"

"Why should you be invited?" said Rakshita.

"After Rimjhim's, we will get married. I'm going to be the future son-in-law of your family," Uma grinned.

"Son-in-law? Have you seen your face?"

"You love me, right?" said Uma authoritatively.

"*Pandey Ji*? Just because I kissed you does not mean I should get married to you. And what are your credentials? You have been preparing for JEE for the past two years, which I doubt you can pass. You are merely a sidekick of Guddu Shukla. You don't have an identity. Do you know my father can find me a suitable match from America? Build your status first, before you think about marriage. *Hum ghoom kya liye tumhare saath, tum to khwaab dekhne lage.*"

Uma was stunned. The tailor of the shop gaped at Uma and Rakshita for a few seconds. Uma's eyes welled up, and he clenched his fist to control his emotions.

"I don't think we should meet anymore," said Rakshita.

Uma left the shop, leaving Rakshita behind. The mall staff in their fluorescent orange t-shirts were hanging an eclectic mix of decorations: Diwali *diyaas*, chandeliers, Christmas wreaths, snowflakes and icicles. The decoration reminded him of Rakshita's behaviour. Now, she had grown cold on him.

Uma thought of asking Rakshita if he could drop her in Barra on his bike. But he decided not to. JEE exams were near, and he had to cover a lot of the syllabus and build his status.

✳

"See, that guy is Bechu," Bechu heard the whisper in Barra Bazaar. Wherever he went in his colony or nearby, he felt that people were staring at him, and they were talking or gossiping about him. He had played these gossips in his mind thousands of times. Bechu Mishra, the murderer. Bechu Mishra, who lived at the mercy of Guddu Shukla. When an enemy hits you, it hurts, but when an enemy shows mercy, it's devastating. In the old days, this could be the reason most kings preferred to be martyred on the battlefield instead of living at the mercy of their nemesis.

He walked fast and saw Tunni's house. Across the road, Gupta's shop was closed, as he had moved to some other place. There were no signs of the auto-walas who used to park their auto in their leisure period too. Bechu thought about Afzal. There was no trace of his *chaat-samosa* cart.

Bechu preferred to wander outside. His house was giving him more pain than the glare or stares he was getting from random people. He thought of meeting Bhujang, but he realized he was not in town. He had gone away for a few weeks. Deemak and Ghosh were absconding after the incident. Bechu wondered if they knew that Guddu had handled the situation, or maybe they were all avoiding Bechu. Now they all knew, Bechu's days were gone. They had found a new hero, Guddu Shukla.

It was late at night, and Bechu strolled back home with a heavy heart. His house was getting painted. Shatrughan Singh had offered to paint the house, and every landlord likes freebies from their tenants. His father had accepted. Bechu wondered, *Why the hell is Rimjhim getting married in my own home?* The wealthy show-off contractor could have booked a big resort or got all the rituals done there. But no, they wanted to wrench his heart till the last drop of love was flushed out. *Stay calm*, he told himself.

He opened the gate and avoided all the decorations that were littered. Within a week, Rimjhim would say a final goodbye. He sighed and clambered on the stairs.

When he entered the house, he saw Shatrughan Singh and his wife, and they were talking about customary approval to use their front yard. Bechu was irked when his father uttered the cliché, "Your daughter is our daughter." A wedding invite was on the table, and Bechu wanted to avoid it, but he read *Nitesh Chauhan weds Rimjhim Singh*.

Bechu went to his room. After five minutes, his room door creaked, and his father entered with a glass of Old Monk in his hand. "How was your exam?" asked Joginder Mishra.

"They were finished weeks ago."

"I know that, but I forgot to ask at the time. How did the papers go?"

"Good."

"Will you pass?"

"Hopefully."

Then Bechu's room clock crawled for a few seconds. His father studied the bedroom, assessed each poster, calendar and picture frame. He saw the picture of Shruti smiling with the rest of the family.

"Papa, the result will come in March. I don't have anything to do in the meantime. I will come to your warehouse and manage the accounts," said Bechu.

"It's okay. I'm not old. Live your life fully. Do whatever you want. Your mother was right, I never gave my time to kids, and I was always busy. I don't show my emotion. But Bechu, remember one thing: if a father does not say 'I love you' to his kids, it is not because he hates them, but because he loves them more." Joginder's eyes were moist. He was in Anupam Kher mode. "I miss Shruti each and every day. Every moment. Now I don't have the courage to miss you too," said Joginder. He took another sip. "I know that girl is getting married. You are my son, and I can read you. I understand your pain. But, let it go. In our life, we have to make decisions for others."

Overcome with sudden emotion, Bechu leapt up and hugged his father. Bechu was also like him, hiding his emotions, bottling them up until they fizzled out and seeped through his eyes.

"I have asked the family to vacate the house after marriage. It's for your sanity. To forget someone quickly, you should keep them out of your sight. I made an excuse that your *chacha* is going to come and live with us so I need that apartment from next month," said Joginder while patting Bechu's back.

Mid-December's cold wave swept Kanpur. Holding a cup of masala tea, Uma revised his physics chapter. Gravitation. He solved a hypothetical problem to calculate the acceleration of gravity, g, for a given mass and radius of a planet. He skimmed through various chapters – gravitation, electricity, magnets. They all reminded him of the word attraction. He thought about Rakshita and decided to get a glimpse of her.

Uma started his bike and drove through Shayam Nagar, Barra. When he arrived in front of the rickety gate around noon, he saw a decorated house. Lights, faux lilies and original marigold flowers. He saw a board reading "Rimjhim Singh weds Nitesh Chauhan."

Uma had not told this to his friend Guddu. He wondered if Guddu knew about this or not. Then he remembered Rakshita's word: Guddu's sidekick. Probably she was right. Or she was wrong. Uma and Guddu had met three years ago at Kanpur Dehat. Both were looking for the same address, Shatrughan Singh. They immediately connected, and Umanath declared himself his *saadhu*, brother-in-law. Uma had helped Guddu to settle in the DAV hostel. They bought a mattress, fridge, TV for his room. Uma always considered him a friend. But probably Guddu looked at Uma as his sidekick. Whatever he was, he had to tell him for the sake of his friendship. He turned his bike towards Civil Lines.

＊

When Uma entered Guddu's room, he saw a new boy, who looked like a fresher, sweeping the floor. He turned pale when he saw Uma.

"Who are you? *Guddu Bhaiya* is not here," said the new guy with trembling hands.

"Where is he?" asked Uma. He noticed the guy's voice. It was hoarse.

"Don't worry, I'm *Guddu Bhaiya's* close friend." Uma opened the fridge and took out a beer bottle, and sipped confidently.

"*Guddu Bhaiya* will come in ten minutes. He has gone to the hospital to see his friend. Some guy has been shifted back from Lucknow to Kanpur's hospital," said the boy.

The word friend was soothing to Uma's ears. He smiled.

"What's your name?"

"I'm Nabin. I'm a first-year student. Moved to the hostel recently," said the new boy.

"My guess is *Guddu Bhaiya* saved you from Vinod Yadav and Rajiv Mahato?"

Nabin lowered his gaze. He looked at the floor and fidgeted with his broom.

"Okay, carry on," said Uma while studying Nabin.

Nabin got busy cleaning Guddu's room and preparing lunch for him. Uma lounged on the sofa, skimmed some magazines – *Outlook, India Today* – and noticed the words and sentences marked and underlined. Next, there was a sheet where Guddu had written a few words and solved some quants questions.

Uma stood up and came out when he heard a Jeep. Footsteps approached room number 21. Sunil and Guddu Shukla entered the room. Guddu beckoned Uma to sit down on the sofa. He went to the kitchen and spat the gutkha in the washbasin.

"Nabin, clean this," Guddu ordered.

"*Bhaiya, naya murga pakad laaye?* Got a new lad?" smirked Uma.

"Seeing you after a long time?" asked Guddu.

"*Bhaiya*, was busy with JEE prep."

"That you have been doing for the past three years."

"This time, I'm serious."

Sunil came and sat down next to Uma. Guddu sat on his fourposter, across from the sofa.

"How is Lala?" asked Uma.

"He is good, recovering. Going through physiotherapy."

"Physiotherapy?"

"Yes, the bullet hit his waistline," said Guddu, and then held his breath for a second. "You leave that. Why is your face so dull? Is there something you want to say?" asked Guddu.

"*Bhaiya*, I'm not sure if you know."

"Know what?"

"That Rimjhim…"

"Rimjhim? What happened to her?" asked Guddu, raising his brow.

"She is getting married."

Sunil Chauhan turned pale, and his shoulders shuddered.

"Getting married, when?"

"Tomorrow," and then Uma's voice faded into silence.

"And you dumb fuck, you are telling me now?!" Guddu shouted. The air seemed heavily and uttering any word worrisome and then his face turned purple. He got up and grabbed Uma's shirt.

"*Guddu Bhaiya*, it's not his mistake," said Sunil Chauhan.

"What do you mean?"

Uma looked at Sunil. He understood what Sunil meant.

"I was aware months ago that Rimjhim is getting married, but I did not tell you. It was my mistake," said Sunil.

Guddu released his grip from Uma's shirt collar. He drew a chair and stared at Sunil.

"Can you explain what's going on?"

"*Guddu Bhaiya*, when Bechu and Bhujang insulted me while playing cricket, I was hurt, and I wanted to take my revenge. My anger was so high that I did not see who was my friend and who was not. I started with Bhujang. To make him jealous, I wooed Tunni, but eventually fell in love. But I was not satisfied. When I came to know Bechu liked Rimjhim. I started thinking about how I could inject more pain into Bechu's heart. I instigated you to propose Rimjhim. Then I took one more step. My cousin who works in America came to India. I spoke to Shatrughan Singh and sent a marriage proposal. My cousin met the family and liked Rimjhim. Anyone would. But, when in the lockup I heard your story, I realized that I had made a mistake. In vengeance, I forgot about you and your love," said Sunil. His voice sank to murmur. He sniffled and hugged Guddu. "I'm sorry *Guddu Bhaiya*. Please forgive me."

"It's okay, don't spoil my shirt," said Guddu.

Sunil was surprised. He thought Guddu may slap him, but Guddu just got up.

"Sunil, you sent the proposal, and now you will break this proposal. *Saale, Apne chachere bhai ki shadi tum aaj rukwaogey.*"

"I did not get you, *Guddu Bhaiya*," asked Uma.

"*Gaadi nikalo be*. I want to meet my father-in-law," said Guddu, tossing his Jeep key towards Nabin. "You two, you're both coming with me." Guddu tucked two loaded pistols into his pants.

※

When the Jeep reached Barra, Shyam Nagar, Guddu waved his hand to stop it. Nabin applied a sudden break. Guddu pulled out his sunglasses and blew on them. He wiped the fog off with his dark blue shirt. He put his glasses back on and jumped out of his Jeep.

"You three, you sit here in the Jeep," instructed Guddu.

Uma, Sunil and Nabin complied in silence. Their throats were dry.

Guddu opened the gate and assessed the situation. He looked around. A few workers were decorating the *mandap* in the front courtyard, and some females were singing a folk song.

"*Band karo yeh taam-jhaam*. Stop this nonsense," roared Guddu.

His voice was so loud that everyone stopped working and singing and looked at Guddu. There was an ominous silence, and a few people ran inside.

"Why should we stop this?" said a tall, stout man in a white kurta and yellow dhoti.

He towered Guddu. It was Shatrughan Singh. Shatrughan's four bodybuilder henchmen surrounded Guddu.

"Contractor Saab, *aapki laundiya se hum pyaar karte hain*. So, she should get married to me," said Guddu. He ignored Shatrughan's men.

"You wait for a minute. I will come back," said Shatrughan. He waved his index finger at Guddu and glared at his men with his red eyes. "Keep him here, make sure he does not run away."

Shatrughan Singh ran inside his house and fetched his double-barrelled rifle. He checked that it was loaded, then came back to the courtyard.

An old man, also in a white kurta and yellow dhoti, patted Shatrughan Singh. His bald pate shined. He combed a few remaining strands of hair over it. "Don't do this, *Babu Saheb*," said Nunu Jha.

"*Pandit ji, Laundey ki himmat dekhiye.* That night, I am sure it was him who catcalled my daughters. Today I will put a bullet in his arse," snarled Shatrughan.

"Do you know who this boy is? He is the son of minister R.C. Shukla. The transport minister. *Gaand main goli aapke lagegi.* Have patience. I will handle it. You go and talk to him nicely," said Nunu Jha. Nunu Jha pulled out a bulky mobile phone from his bag and held the bag under his arm. With one hand, he dialled a number.

Bechu heard the commotion and looked out from his window. He saw the familiar Jeep and Guddu standing in his own front yard. Bechu frowned, and he rummaged his cupboard to pick a gun. He zipped his jacket and marched towards the door.

"*Beta dekho,*" said Shatrughan in a softened tone.

"*Kaka, hamey na dikhao.* You should listen to *Guru Ji,* Nunu Jha's advice. I have decided. Stop this, else I will kidnap your daughter."

"What are you doing here?" Guddu heard a loud voice asking – it was Bechu.

"Oh, welcome. We missed you. Didn't you see it on the TV news? I came here to stop this marriage," Guddu mocked.

"Guddu, go away. Last time I missed my aim, but this time, I won't," said Bechu. He flashed his pistol and put his finger on the trigger.

"Oh, looks like you have practised well. Then shoot. Let's decide on the spot," said Guddu, and he spread his arms dramatically.

Guddu's mobile phone rang. He looked around and noticed a winning smile on Nunu Jha's face. He answered the call.

"Wherever you are, stop everything and come home," R.C. Shukla said on the phone.

"But *Babuji*…"

"If there is any respect left in your heart for me, come home. I will take care of everything, trust me. And yes, come with the girl's father."

Guddu hung up the phone and gave Bechu a disgusted look. He turned towards the Jeep and shouted at his friends, "Start it. *Ab darbaar kahin aur lagegi*. We are going to Lucknow."

✳

Guddu's feet became numb on the cold white marble floor. He and his friends had driven for three hours to reach Lucknow. Guddu had asked them to wait on the patio of his bungalow.

Shatrughan Singh and Nunu Jha had sunk on the sofa across from R.C. Shukla. A waiter attired in white served tea. Shatrughan Singh gaped at the big drawing hall. He noticed a big portrait of a man hanging on the wall. It was K.C. Shukla, ex-chief minister of UP and grandfather of Guddu.

Shatrughan Singh removed a handkerchief from his breast pocket and wiped the sweat off his head. "Guddu is a very nice boy, *Shukla Ji*. If our castes were the same, I would not mind. *Humey koi aitraaz nahi hota*," said Shatrughan Singh.

"*Aitraaz dikha ke aap kuch kar bhi nahi sakte Singh sahab*. You cannot do anything," said R.C. Shukla. He had the same tone and attitude as Guddu. "I use the caste card in politics, not in family matters."

"Guddu, do you like the girl?" R.C. Shukla looked at his son and smiled.

"Yes, Babuji," Guddu nodded.

"And I assume the girl likes you?" asked R.C. Shukla.

"That… that… that I don't know," stammered Guddu.

That was true. Rimjhim never expressed her feeling, and she was always terrified of Guddu. Her eyes had said it many times, but Guddu always ignored this. Guddu could have forced himself on her, but he knew he could not win her heart.

"If the girl does not like you, then why are you forcing yourself on her? What do you want? Should I behave like other ministers and help you kidnap the girl and marry her to you forcefully?" said R.C. Shukla calmly. He turned to Shatrughan Singh. "You can go. Get your daughter married with great festivity. He will not do anything."

"It would be great if you provided some police guards for security."

"That won't be needed. You take my number, call me anytime if help is needed," R.C. Shukla beckoned his PA.

Guddu did not say a word. He realized it was similar to the conversation he had had with his father in the police station. "*If I was acting like a politician's kid, I would not have been here for a small brawl. Maybe I would have been here for a rape case.*" This is what he had said to his father.

Guddu looked at the portrait of his grandfather; politics had been in his family for generations. Once more, he had succumbed to it.

21

The mid-December air was suffocating. Bechu could hear the brass band that was approaching his house. He had locked himself in his room. Bechu tried to cover his ears with the pillow, but it did not help. To avoid the glittering decorating lights, he had covered his windows with newspaper. But still, a faint beam of light was coming in. It was unbearable. Home is not a place, but it's a feeling. Bechu was feeling like a stranger in his own house.

His first love – and perhaps his last – was getting married to someone else in his own courtyard. He cursed his fate. With a heavy heart, he picked up a pen and began to write.

"I'm not a writer, so I don't know how to express my emotions. You are getting married, so I have to write a customary sentence first – happy married life.

For my feelings, I think the following lyrics can express them better.

> *Mubarakein tumhe ke tum kisi ke noor ho gaye,*
> *Kisi ke itne paas ho ke sabse door ho gaye."*

Bechu folded the paper and put it in an envelope. He handed it to Chotu and whispered in his ear.

When he came out of the house, he saw Rakshita. She avoided eye contact with him and ran towards the gate with a few other giggling girls. One of them screamed, "*Baaraat aa gayi.*" Young girls and women ran and climbed the stairs to get a better view from the first floor of Bechu's house. Men took their position at the gate with a marigold garland in their hands.

"*Beta*, you are also part of the family. Take this garland and be ready to welcome the bridegroom's family," said Shatrughan Singh when he saw Bechu. He gave a weird look when he saw that Bechu was in his regular clothes.

Bechu took it reluctantly. A pain shuddered in his chest, and he felt he could not breathe. He looked aside. He saw Deemak, Ghosh, and Bhujang at the food counter, lending their helping hands as good colony boys. Bhujang gave him a look: "You still have time," it urged.

✳

Chotu peered through the crowd and went inside the bride's room. Most of the girls were busy watching the approaching *baaraat,* where the boys were performing Nagin dance. Chotu gave the envelope to Rimjhim. She looked stunning in a dark maroon lehenga. Rimjhim opened the letter, and tears rolled down her cheeks.

✳

When the *baaraat* came at the gate, a few guys rejected the idea of getting welcomed. They saw the girls on the first floor and started dancing hysterically. One guy became *sapera* and others five *naags*. They slithered on the dusty road. The band-wala had been playing "been" music for more than ten minutes when Bechu got frustrated. He forcefully peered through the *baaraatis*, abused a few dancers, and put the welcome garland on the stunned bridegroom. A few more followed.

"Bechu, you should not misbehave with the in-law's family," said Shatrughan Singh.

"They are your in-laws, not mine," glared Bechu, and he vanished down the dark road.

Bhujang, Deemak and Ghosh started distributing welcome drinks.

✳

"*Babuji* is a true politician," said Guddu.

Guddu poured some *namkeen* on different paper plates. DAV hostel was almost empty. In December, there were no university classes, so students had gone to their hometowns. Some were still absconding after Lala's injury.

"Vinod Yadav has joined *Babuji's* party," Guddu informed his friends.

"What? This is so unfair. And what about you?"

"He wants to send me to Australia. La Trobe University, for my MBA."

"Are you going?" asked Sunil.

Guddu nodded his head. He took a deep drag of *ganja* and twitched his right shoulder. He looked at Nabin and beckoned him, and Nabin poured "*Navratan Tel*" in his palm and started massaging Guddu's head.

"*Guddu Bhaiya*, I'm sorry," said Sunil. He sipped his glass of whisky.

"I don't forgive people," Guddu looked at Sunil. "Today is the last day of our friendship. So enjoy it, and from tomorrow, never again show your face here," said Guddu. He closed his eyes when Nabin's fingers ran through his hair.

Sunil looked down. He stared at the glass.

"What are you doing here anyway? Go attend your cousin's marriage. They might be looking for you!" said Guddu.

Uma took another sip. He was fixated on his "*namkeen plate.*" After a few minutes, he raised his index finger like a wise man. "*Bhaiya, ek baat samajh nahi aayi.* I'm missing one point here," said Uma with a twinkle in his eyes.

"What is that?" asked Guddu. He took one more drag.

"Bechu… Bechu loves Rimjhim but…"

Guddu got to his feet. He took his leather jacket and wrapped a scarf around his neck. "Even I have the same question in my mind. Let's go," said Guddu.

"Where?" asked Uma.

"*Aakhiri kand karney.* My last ritual is incomplete. Let's go to Barra, Shyam Nagar."

"But R.C Shukla had asked us to stay away…" said Uma

"*Netaji* asked us not to disturb the marriage. He did not say we cannot join the celebrations."

✳

Guddu drove fast on Hamirpur road. It was around 10:00 pm night, thus there was no sign of traffic. Nabin held his seat tightly, and Uma, in the front seat, felt the wind dishevel his hair. Uma noticed that Guddu was still carefree. Today his love Rimjhim was getting married, but he was not anxious. Holding the beer bottle, Uma felt confident, and it reminded him of his old days with Guddu.

"*Bhaiya,* don't do anything. They are my family members, and my parents, *bua, chacha-chachi* all are there," said Sunil.

"*Abye chutiye,* I'm not going to murder your cousin, neither am I going to meet Rimjhim. Don't worry," said Guddu.

When he took a turn towards Shyam Nagar, he saw a familiar boy sitting in the darkness. It was Bechu.

Guddu saw Bechu, and he stopped his Jeep. Bechu saw him coming towards him. Bechu took a cigarette packet from his pocket, which he had bought a few minutes ago from Pan Shop; he took one and lit it. He looked up at the starlit sky. Orion and big dipper were shining upon him. Treacherously bright. Star positions were not helping his fate. There was a chill in the air and a vast emptiness in his life...

"It's better to fall off a bridge than falling in love... It hurts less," said Guddu as he approached Bechu.

Bechu ignored the familiar voice. Guddu's clear voice rose and then fell. Some other feeling was struggling within him and he did not even look at Guddu. For him now, life was meaningless. Once you have a broken heart, there is no escape. Now, each breath was an effort.

"Go away," said Bechu when he heard Guddu's footsteps a few feet away.

Guddu noticed the flare of the cigarette. "*Kya kar rahe ho apni sulga ke.* I know you are smouldering like this cigarette," said Guddu.

"I have nothing to say," Bechu took a drag and then glared at Guddu.

"So, you don't have any grudge against me?"

"My life does not have a place for you. Don't give yourself so much importance," said Bechu.

"Why? I think you should hate me," asked Guddu surprised.

"Huh!" Bechu chuckled. "Guddu, for a moment, remove yourself from this story and look at my life. You will not find any difference. I might have still flunked my CA exams, my fate will be the same..." said Bechu. He looked at the thin traffic of Barra Bazar Chowk, then looked at Guddu. "You know Guddu? You have a habit of imposing yourself on others to feel that the world revolves around you. You tried to impose yourself on Rimjhim. Now you are trying to win and impose your story on me. But look, my story would have been the same without you. I'm a loser. Your presence will not make me a winner."

Bechu looked away trying to hide the tears from his welling eyes.

For the first-time Guddu's heart felt weak. Bechu was right. He had always tried to force his presence on Rimjhim, Lala, and his father, now Bechu. If Bechu was a loser, that made him a loser too. Guddu took the cigarette from Bechu's hand and took a deep drag.

"Then come, and let's celebrate. We both lost the semi-final," Guddu sneered. He came forward, put his hand on Bechu's shoulder and patted. "It's okay. We both lost. We are losers. We are now bonded by the same thread. Losers are brothers. Now come on, buckle up."

Bechu could not control himself any longer. He stood up and hugged him; the carefully held tears finally brimming over. He needed it. He needed a friend now who could stand with him and say it was all okay. Guddu held him in a tight embrace for a couple of minutes, wondering all the while, where he was gaining the strength to stay this calm; in reality, he did not feel much different from the way Bechu did.

"Do you want to see the final?" asked Guddu handing Bechu a handkerchief. "Wipe your face, my friends are there in the Jeep and I don't want them to see that a tiger can cry."

✳

"No *Bhaiya*, I cannot do this," said Sunil.

"This is the last thing I'm asking. You were looking for forgiveness, and you will get it," said Guddu.

Guddu parked his Jeep some distance away. The sound of the *shehnaai* was paining his heart more than his ears.

"Look, your relatives are at the marriage, we just want to use the terrace. Bring some whisky and food. We will all witness our love interest's marriage from your *Bua's* rooftop."

Sunil gulped his spit. Uma took the Jeep keys from Guddu. "You guys got to the terrace. I will arrange things," he muttered.

✳

They all had a glass of whisky in hand. Uma lit a bonfire, and the yellow light glowed everyone's face. Guddu drew Bechu closer and pointed his index finger towards a decorated house, which was Bechu's.

"That's the final match, getting played on your turf," said Guddu.

Bechu looked at his own house. Some tears seeped into his eyes. He thought about mentioning the letter he wrote to Rimjhim, but he did not. He looked around. He was surrounded by strange faces, which were his new friends. He did not want to open up to them. He did not want to be close to anyone. He wished Rishabh was there. Bechu stared at the '*mandap*' where Rimjhim was going around the fire, the *saat phere*, of her wedding. Bechu did not blink for a second for the next five minutes. he was standing like a stone... Motionless, lifeless. The others looked at him in silence.

"I do not understand one thing. You did not oppose the marriage! *Prem kartey ho baakir shadi main ungli nahi kiya tumne?*" asked Guddu.

"I wanted to see her happy, and she is getting married to a nice guy. Better than us," said Bechu dabbing his misty eyes.

Hearing and witnessing the philosophy about love, Guddu became serious. He looked at his glass again. The neat whiskey was turning him to Socrates.

"Why do we always look for love in places where we are never going to get it?" Guddu asked. He was feeling equally shattered and wretched but he chose not to show or express it further.

"Your question has the answer. If you try to get something, you are not looking for love. You are looking for achievement," said Bechu.

"Sachin Tendulkar, *ishq ke Sachin Tendulkar ho tum*," shouted Guddu in a wistful manner. He raised his whisky glass dramatically. "But, unfortunately, you got out at 99, and you missed the century. Big fan. Now, I am your fan. Look at my love. It was like Vinod Kambli. My love was not love. It was…" Guddu struggled to find a suitable word. He looked to Uma for help.

"Lust!" said Uma.

"*Chup kar bey*, I know English. I'm a future La Trobe student," said Guddu. He thought for a few more seconds and screamed, "Infatuation… my love was not love but an infatuation. But your love was *Ishq*."

"*Bhaiya*. There is a song by Madonna on infatuation," said Sunil.

"We are not looking for your suggestions anymore," frowned Uma. "A lot goes behind your innocent face that does not come out in your talk."

"Uma, keep quiet. I'm talking about my love here," Guddu hissed. "I have been pretending to be something I'm not. I'm from Lucknow, and from now, I will be like them," said Guddu. He took another sip. "Do you guys know about

Mir Taqi Mir? He was a poet from Lucknow. I recall a *sher*, couplet, from him, that goes,

> *shifa apni taqdir hi men na thi*
> *ki maqdur tak to dava kar chale*

"*Waah, waah,*" shouted Uma, as he poured whisky in his glass.

Guddu sat on the floor. For him, it was a queer feeling to call his love a mere infatuation. But he had to do it. He had to show that he was not a loser. He never liked being a loser.

Uma gulped his fourth whisky and started crying. He crawled towards the railing, managed to stand and looked towards Bechu's house.

"*Rakhista, humko chodd ke kyun chali gayi?* Why did you dump me?" Umanath screamed.

"Shut up, you *rondlu aashiq*. A cry baby," said Guddu. Guddu held Bechu's hand and pulled him towards the bonfire. Sunil came forward for help as Guddu stumbled. Guddu pushed him away.

"Clean your rooftop before your relative comes back from the marriage," Guddu ordered. And then Guddu put his hand on Bechu's shoulder and looked into his eyes. "Bechu, my brother. I am taking an oath while touching this marvellous ornated bottle of single malt: one day, I will find a girl for you. I promise you. You will get married to your dream girl."

Umanath rolled on the floor, and the whisky bottle shattered.

Current Date

The flight stewards announced the descent, and it ended Guddu, aka Himanshu's sleep. He rubbed his eyes and looked outside the window. He saw tiny houses and roads where the traffic was speeding.

Twenty minutes after the pilot's announcement, flight AI411 landed. Guddu came out from the flight and waited at the door.

Rimjhim came, and she looked around. Guddu waved and strolled towards Rimjhim.

"Coffee?" asked Guddu.

"Sure. Should we first collect our baggage?" asked Rimjhim. She looked for the way to exit.

"Follow me. I can show you the way."

Rimjhim did so. At the airport newspaper stand, she saw the flashing news about the UP elections on the TV.

"So, do you think R.C. Shukla can be the new chief minister? His party may win the election," asked Rimjhim.

"He is old, but he can be," said Guddu.

Guddu peered at Rimjhim's face, to read if she knew R.C. Shukla was his father. He looked at the TV, and Vinod Yadav, the current education minister, was standing behind R.C. Shukla, supporting his CM candidature.

"I don't follow politics," said Guddu.

"Looks like you travel a lot – you know all the gates and exits."

"Yes, I am a frequent flyer," said Guddu. "This way," he led.

They reached the Terminal A baggage carousel. Rimjhim identified her red stroller bag, and Guddu pulled it off and placed it on the trolley.

"So, time for coffee? There is a Starbucks at the corner."

Rimjhim smiled and followed him. Guddu had never thought that in the future, he would be drinking coffee with her. Destiny takes us on different paths, and we cannot guess how it's going to cross.

Guddu ordered a tall pike for himself and a latte for Rimjhim.

"After marriage, you disappeared," said Guddu.

"My family moved to Lucknow, and I was in the US for a few years. What about you? Did you complete IIM?"

"No, I did my MBA in Australia. La Trobe."

"Fancy."

"What do you do?" asked Guddu.

"I'm a Sanskrit professor here at Satyawati College."

"I know it's a tough subject. I've attended few classes," Guddu grinned. "But with a teacher like you, it should be easy."

Rimjhim blushed. Guddu looked outside to get a glimpse of the sky.

"It's going to rain. I hope your husband arrives on time to pick you up."

Rimjhim lowered her gaze, and she scratched at the chipping paint on the chair for a moment. Her lips quivered. "He died in a road accident in Minnesota. I came back in 2007 and completed my master's, then appeared for the NET exam. I have been working here in Delhi for the past thirteen years."

"Oh, I'm so sorry," said Guddu. A feeling of regret ran up his spine.

"It's okay. You don't need to look remorseful."

"My friend is coming. He will be here in a few minutes. I will drop you then."

"No, I will take an Uber," said Rimjhim. She took out her smartphone from her Michael Kors bag and touched the screen for the app.

"I insist. *Isi bahaney,* we will get an opportunity to talk more."

"But, I live in the opposite direction. I'm not going to Delhi. I live in Noida, sector 11."

"That's better," said Guddu. His face split with a smile. "I live in Noida too, sector 52. So technically, we are still *UP-wallahs.*"

"Okay."

Guddu took Rimjhim's trolley and walked towards the exit gate.

✳

After a few minutes of waiting in the Delhi drizzle, a white Audi Q5 arrived. Like a gentleman, Guddu ran to open the door of the backseat and beckoned Rimjhim to sit.

Rimjhim noticed a man dressed not like Chunky Pandey, but Daniel Craig. He stepped out from the driver's seat. A dusky petite girl in sunglasses was next to him. Rimjhim gasped and chuckled like a child.

"Uma Pandey?" shouted Rimjhim, jumping to her feet. She could not recognize the second girl – it must be Uma's girlfriend. Uma was astonished. She looked at Guddu, bewildered.

"You are married, *Bhaiya* and today is Sanaya's birthday. How come? Are you going to give her this gift?" Uma muttered.

"Don't worry, Uma. Guddu is an absolute gentleman. He flirts a little, but he knows his boundaries," said Rimjhim.

"Oh, sorry if I was loud. I meant…" stammered Uma.

"It's fine. It was my mistake that I eavesdropped. So how have you been?"

Oh… yes. Myself Uma Nath Pandey, Computer Science topper, IIT Delhi 2008. Currently working as a CTO of a startup," said Uma in his peculiar style.

Rimjhim smiled. She took a seat in the back and then tried to recognize the dusky girl again. She was in a scarlet top and a black mini skirt. She stared back at Rimjhim.

"Do I know you?" asked Rimjhim

"You did not recognize her?" asked Guddu, taking a seat next to Rimjhim.

Rimjhim looked carefully. Her face was familiar, then the girl extended her hand.

"*Rimjhim di*, it's me, Khusbu. Tunni," Tunni smiled.

"Oh, you have changed so much. Sorry," said Rimjhim, fixing her eyes on Tunni. She looked prettier than before. "I did not know that you and Uma knew each other, Uma and…." Rimjhim hesitated further. She wanted to talk about her sister Rakshita but did not speak further.

"No no, we are not dating. I cracked JEE in 2003 and got admission in Delhi. Uma joined one year after. So I was his senior. As we both were from Kanpur and knew each other a little, we became friends," said Tunni and winked at Uma.

"Tunni, I mean Khushi lives in San Francisco with a live-in partner. She is a product manager at Yahoo. She came here on vacation for a month and helped us with this startup product requirements."

"Ignore this. How is Sunil?" asked Guddu to Rimjhim, and then he looked at Tunni and smirked. He has started enjoying teasing Tunni with the names of her past lovers or admirers.

"That's not fair," said Tunni.

"Fair? All the *chaat-wallah, magazine-wallah and auto-wallah* used to be your fans. We are at least teasing you with the right prospect. Should we start with Bhujang? He is now a celebrity fitness guru. He is running a YouTube channel and helping the skinny models of Delhi to build a strong core," smirked Uma.

"You should meet him, Khushi. Maybe he will help you to tone your body for free," said Guddu.

"No thanks. It has been seventeen years. You and *Bechu Bhaiya* always tease me." Tunni reacted.

Rimjhim shifted in her seat and wrung her fingers. She looked out in nervousness and read the sign "Welcome to Noida." Her heart jolted when she heard Bechu's name.

"Sunil is doing well. He retired from the Indian Army and got a corporate job as a senior manager in Ahmadabad. Tunni, do you need his number?" said Rimjhim.

"How come you know about Sunil?" asked Tunni.

"He is my husband's cousin."

"Ohh. I was not aware of that. I was a young girl then. It was puppy love," said Tunni and turned her head. She looked at Rimjhim, who was avoiding the conversation. "Love comes with maturity. Teenage love is always immature and stupid. Isn't it *Rimjhim di*?"

Rimjhim looked at Tunni, her lips curled. She held her Hindi novel tight. Guddu noticed the novel writer's name the first time.

"Okay, Tunni, we won't tease you anymore. Let's start with Uma, then?" said Guddu.

"Why me? You don't have anything to pull my legs," said Uma

"We have," said Guddu and turned towards Rimjhim. "How is Rakshita?"

Rimjhim smiled. "She is doing fine. Married to a techie. She is in Australia."

"Oh, so sad," Tunni turned towards Uma and tried to touch his cheek.

"Stop it. But I'm not like you, Khushi. I still stalk my unrequited love on Facebook," Uma smiled.

"That's the problem with you guys. You are stuck in the past. Move on."

"Are you ready to leave your live-in boyfriend and marry me? Then I will move on," said Uma.

"Stop flirting. I know you are learning this from *Guddu Bhaiya*. He is terrible at it," said Tunni.

The car turned at sector eleven, and GPS announced that the destination was ten minutes away. A song crackled on the radio. Rimjhim's lips quivered, but she took a deep breath. "Can you increase the volume?" she said.

Uma quickly obliged. Rimjhim closed her eyes.

'*Yeh Roshni Ke Saath Kyun, Dhuan Utha Chirag Se,
Yeh Khwaab Dekhti Hoon Main, Ke Jag Padi Hoon
Khwaab Se*'

Guddu stared at Rimjhim for the next five minutes, and no one spoke till the song ended. The silence was so intense that he could hear the rhythm of Rimjhim's heartbeat. The car took another turn, and GPS showed five more minutes to destination.

"Time to say goodbye," Tunni said to Rimjhim.

"Yes, but Tunni – sorry, Khushi, I disagree," said Rimjhim

"Disagree with what?" Tunni turned back.

"That young love is stupid and immature. Love can happen at any age, and when you feel that it was a mistake, it was not love. It was a mere attraction. And even after seventeen years, if you feel the love, if you long for it, you know it was pure and pious." Rimjhim looked out the window. "Uma, just to the left and stop. That yellow building is my apartment building."

Guddu opened the door for Rimjhim and picked up her luggage. He rummaged in his pocket, pulled out a visiting card, and handed it to Rimjhim.

"This has my number," said Guddu.

"Himanshu Shukla," said Rimjhim while reading the card. "Is that your name?"

"*Puri zindagi Kanpur ki galiyon main aapke peeche daudtey rahe*. I spent half of my life pursuing you, and you don't even know my name?" Guddu sneered.

"No, I was aware of Guddu Shukla."

"Anyways, type in your number, let's be in touch," Guddu handed his mobile to Rimjhim. Rimjhim stored her number in his phone. She saw Sanaya's picture as wallpaper.

"She is beautiful," said Rimjhim.

✳

"What was that?" Tunni asked when Guddu took his seat.

"What? I was showing some chivalry," said Guddu.

"Not that *Guddu Bhiaya*. She is asking about the final lecture from her on love. Looks like she was pissed off," Uma said.

"No, stupid. She is still in love," said Tunni.

"In love, but with whom?" asked Uma.

"Ah, God knows how you cracked JEE," said Tunni, raising her brow.

"With Amit Mishra – I mean, Bechu Mishra," said Guddu.

"How come? Are you sure?" asked Uma.

Tunni saw a *chai-waalah* beside the road.

"Can you stop the car? I will explain it over tea," said Tunni.

Uma pulled the car over, and they ordered three masala chai.

"See, I am a girl, and my intuition says she still loves *Bechu Bhaiya*. Did you notice how she clinched her sweaty palm when she first heard Bechu's name? I could see the longing for him in her eyes," said Tunni.

"And this song… '*Ajeeb dastan hai yeh*', Bechu had told this story thousands of times after drinks. That he wrote this song and gave it to her," Guddu added.

"So?" Tunni turned towards Guddu.

"So what?"

"*Bhaiya*, today is Sanaya and Bechu's birthday. Invite her. Don't tell her Bechu is coming. Let's unite the love birds," said Tunni excitedly.

"Don't you guys know that Rimjhim is taller than Bechu? How come a tall girl can fall in love with a short guy," asked Uma.

"Are you serious? In the era when Priyanka is married to Nick Jonas or Tom Cruise dated and married girls taller than him, you are still stuck that idea that this cannot happen?" asked Tunni.

"No, but they are celebrities," said Uma.

"Look at you. Girls don't hang out with dumb and stupid guys. Still, I talk to you, Mr Pandey," Tunni warned and giggled. "Ignore him, *Guddu Bhaiya*. Let's do it."

Guddu picked up his phone and dialled the recently stored number. After multiple rings, it went to the voice mailbox.

"Hi, Rimjhim. It is Guddu here. Look, tonight we are celebrating my wife's birthday at Tito's. It's in Noida. Can you be there at 8:00 PM? We all will be waiting for you."

Guddu scrolled through his contacts on mobile and dialled another number.

"Who are you calling now?" asked Uma.

"I have to ask one more person to join the party. That story also needs closure," said Guddu. He looked outside of the car windows. A few hawkers were selling pirated books. "Uma, can you drop me at DLF mall at Noida. I need to attend an event there. Drop my bags at home. I will talk to Sanaya." He turned to Tunni. "Khushi, see you at Tito's tonight."

There was a small gathering at "Book World" in DLF mall. When Guddu entered the books store, he immediately found the person he was looking for. A guy in the wheelchair was signing books. A few readers asked questions about the future of Hindi Sahitya and how Nayi Hindi impacted the market.

Guddu picked a copy of the novel from the bookstall. It was '*Kanpur Wala Love*', by Animesh Srivastava – the same Hindi novel Rimjhim was reading.

The author managed to sign some more books quickly and pushed his wheelchair towards Guddu. "*Guddu Bhaiya*, thanks for coming. I didn't think you would be able to make it," said the author.

"Lala, how could I avoid attending my roommate's book signing event?" said Guddu. He hesitated to say "roommate", then he flipped the last few pages of the novel. "Congratulations," said Guddu.

"Thanks, *Bhaiya*. Roommate?" Lala smiled at the word.

"I have a question related to this novel, and I need an honest answer."

"I'm alive because of you. Finally, my dream came true. Ask anything. I think I know what you are going to ask."

"Don't show any gratitude to me, Lala. I'm not worth it," said Guddu. "This novel is based on our college time story, right?"

"Partially, yes, but I have changed all names and locations," said Lala.

"So who gets the heroine? The character resembling Guddu Shukla or Bechu Mishra?"

"Neither, my novel ends when the female protagonist gets married."

"That's the writers' dramatic ending. What should be the real ending?" asked Guddu.

"I don't know. In reality, this is what happens. The girl gets married to someone else. Drama happens only in movies."

"What if I can twist the story. If I can reunite the lovers?"

"Can you? You are not god, *Guddu Bhaiya*. You can only try," said Lala like a philosopher and shrugged.

"Do you know, Rimjhim was reading your book."

"This book came onto the market last week, and she gets her copy so soon?" asked Lala, surprised. "She must have pre-ordered. Is she still keeping a tab on us?"

"Probably yes. She loves Bechu, I'm sure. Lala, be ready to write a sequel," Guddu smirked, and he gave a book to Lala. "Can I get a signed copy?"

Lala signed with a broad smile. Guddu pulled out a credit card from his wallet to buy the book.

"No need, *Guddu Bhaiya*. You have always given me a lot. This is a gift from your roommate," Lala stressed the word 'roommate'.

"Okay, I have to leave. But one thing you should never forget, the person who chases his dream facing all different challenges is the real hero. And the real hero of the story is you, Lala. It's you."

Guddu left the bookshop immediately. He liked Lala a lot, but he could never meet his eyes or talk much with him. He felt guilty that Lala was leading a differently-abled life, in a wheelchair, because of Guddu and his stupidity. Yes, Guddu could not be a god. He had spent money on Lala's medical bills to fix his problems, but he could not bring his life back to normal. The bullet had hit his spine, made him crippled for life, but Lala never blamed him or Bechu. He never complained. He always smiled at his pain and chased his dream, and finally, he achieved it. Facing all adversity, he published his first book and started his career as a novelist. He was a hero.

Guddu came out from the DLF mall with misty and prideful eyes and called for an auto. He had made a decision to mend some mistakes of the past. It was a time to take the next decisive step.

✻

Uma and Tunni moved their hips on the dance floor as the DJ played "Hips Don't Lie". She was in a dark blue ensemble, and the pearls around her neck were glittering in the fluorescent disco lights. Tunni moved her body closer to Uma's crotch, and Uma felt himself begin to sweat. Tunni's perfume made him nervous. Or it could be pheromones. She was attractive. Her sweaty smell smeared with Chanel could bring erection even to guys struggling with ED.

Guddu ordered six tequila shots.

"Why six? We are only five," Sanaya, Guddu's wife, frowned.

"I'm expecting guests," Guddu smiled.

Uma and Tunni came to their designated lounge, which was a reserved VIP area. Six tequila shots arrived at the table with lime and salt.

"Remember, lick, shoot and suck," bellowed Tunni above the noise.

"Yes, Miss New York," said Bechu.

"I'm from San Francisco," Tunni shouted.

"No, you are from Kanpur Barra," said Uma and clung to her.

Guddu, Sanaya, Uma, Bechu and Tunni applied salt to their hands.

"For good times," Tunni toasted the glass.

They all licked the salt, drank the shot swiftly, and finished it by sucking on a wedge of lime. Guddu beckoned the waiter to bring cakes, and Uma hugged Tunni after the tequila shot.

"You guys should date and get married. Tunni, dump your live-in partner," said Sanaya.

"No, he is not my type. I don't date my juniors," said Tunni, and she winked at Uma.

"Hello, miss US, in age, I'm elder to you. I just took a few extra years to complete JEE, and I had my reasons," said Uma.

"Whatever," Tunni teased.

"Bechu. What about you? When are you getting married?" asked Sanaya.

"Same answer, I have not found my type yet," Bechu smiled.

After a few minutes, cakes arrived.

"Wait, guys, I ordered two cakes. One is Tres leches, and the other is Tiramisu," said Tunni excitedly.

"What are these?" asked Bechu.

"Tres leches is for you. Tiramisu is an aphrodisiac. Get married if you want to eat," Tunni's eyes twinkled.

"What is aphrodisiac now, and why are you guys talking about my marriage? For that, I need to find a girl," said Bechu.

"For the meaning of aphrodisiac, google *Amit Bhaiya*. If you have a girlfriend, you have to know good aphrodisiac food," said Tunni. She raised her finger to advise all the guys of the group.

"I bet you will find your dream girl today, so you can taste it," Guddu smirked, looking at his mobile screen. After checking the word meaning in an online dictionary, he looked at his WhatsApp messages. His eyes scanned the bar area. There must be traffic outside, he thought.

"Okay, guys, let's cut the cake," shouted Tunni again. She lit the candles on the Tiramisu, and Sanaya picked up the knife.

"Wait," said Guddu. He rummaged in his suit pants and pulled out a small box. He opened it and bent his knee.

"We met sixteen years ago at La Trobe University. My heart had bruises, and you mended it like a perfect doctor. You were the girl who understood me. You were able to read my mind. Later I realised it's because you were doing a master's in psychology," Guddu grinned. "Thank you for everything you've brought into my life. After six years of courtship, you married me. Kudos to you for enduring my rants for ten years. Here" – Guddu showed the diamond ring and waved it – "for celebrating your tenth birthday after marriage. A small token from me." Guddu slipped a diamond ring on Sanaya's fingers.

Sanaya put both hands over her mouth. She gave a small peck on Guddu's cheek and shoved the piece of Tiramisu in Guddu's mouth. They kissed.

"Okay, now It's *Bechu Bhaiya's* turn," said Tunni clapping her hands. She looked at Guddu.

Guddu again checked his watch. It was 9:00 PM. He had reserved the place only till 10:00, and he had one hour left. Anticipating that the invited guest may not come, he beckoned Tunni to continue.

Then Guddu heard a murmur. A guy in the suit stood near the reserved lounge, checking with waiters for Himanshu Shukla. He was holding a bouquet.

Bechu looked at the guy, and he was shocked.

"Yes, it's Rishabh. Forget everything. Go hug him," said Guddu.

Bechu ran and hugged Rishabh. He was meeting him after seventeen years. His eyes were moist.

"I'm sorry," said Bechu.

"I should be sorry. I came late," said Rishabh, stressing the word "late". He held Bechu's head and tousled his hair. "Come, let's cut the cake."

Sanaya and Tunni chukled. Bechu picked up a knife to cut the cake. Guddu looked at his mobile again, and he saw a message alert.

"Wait," Guddu shouted.

"What's happened now?" asked Bechu.

"There is a surprise birthday gift for you."

"*Ab kitna surprise dega.* How many are hidden?" said Bechu.

"Look at that corner," said Guddu, and he pointed his index finger.

A woman was standing in a yellow sari. An avalanche started in Bechu's heart, and everything became slow. Thousands of butterflies with curiosities somersaulted in his stomach. He looked at Guddu in surprise and saw him grin and nod. His voice choked. It was his best birthday gift. He cut the cake, picked up a piece, and walked towards the woman in the yellow sari.

Guddu clapped and felt content. "It's Tiramisu, Italians believe that it's aphrodisiac," he shouted and whistled using his fingers.

A tiny droplet of happiness trickled down from Rimjhim's eyes. Eventually, she had found her love.

About the Author

Ashwini Rudra was born and raised in Arrah, a small town sixty kilometres from the state capital of Bihar, Patna. He received his elementary education in Arrah and Patna. In 2007 he completed his Engineering Degree from VTU and moved to the U.S. (Groton, Connecticut) thereafter, to work with a pharmaceutical company to develop applications for life scientists. Living in solitude for more than a year, he started creating and weaving stories for killing time. Later, it became his passion.

Delhi via Lucknow is his debut novel. His first book, a Hindi story collection, Amerikistan, was an Amazon bestseller. Currently, he lives in Matawan, a small town in New Jersey. He claims to be a simple man with a small-town attitude for life which he intends never to shed.

www.ashwinirudra.com

Ashwini Rudra is a public speaker, and he is available for speaking engagements. To inquire about possible speaking appearances, please contact him at ashwinirudra@outlook.com

You can also follow Ashwini on social media:

- : @RudraAshwini
- : the.humpty.writer
- : rudra.ashwini.1

Made in United States
North Haven, CT
02 August 2022